The
Bay Psalm Book
MURDER

 *Will Harriss*

WALKER AND COMPANY ✸ NEW YORK

First published in the United States of America
in 1983 by the Walker Publishing Company, Inc.

Published simultaneously in Canada by John Wiley & Sons
Canada, Limited, Rexdale, Ontario.

ISBN: 0-8027-5494-5

Library of Congress Catalog Card Number: 82-51306

Printed in the United States of America

10 9 8 7 6 5 4 3 2 1

ONE

No, it was impossible, Cliff Dunbar decided. No student at Los Angeles University could possibly be more glad than he was that June had come at last and the school year was over. Not that he *felt* glad. "Glad" was the wrong word. Jesus, what a year! Bracketed by his wife's death from cancer at one end and his friend's murder at the other.

Well, his resignation from the English Department closed the book on all that. He was free now, in the same sense that Robinson Crusoe was free when he crawled exhausted onto the sands of Selkirk Island. And as lonely.

Carole was gone—early last September, a week before the academic year began. My God, who ever heard of cancer metastasizing that fast? Lung cancer at that, and Carole hadn't even smoked. Cliff had—still did. He wondered uneasily if psychiatrists would say he had a death wish, that he wanted to join Carole. Chilling thought.

And dear old, grouchy, skeptical, brilliant Link Schofield, murdered last month in the garage of his apartment building. It was the kind of story that was becoming all too common in Los Angeles: two young hoodlums knifing a great librarian with forty years experience. And for what? A miserable fourteen dollars! Damn, but life can be cruel. His wife and his best friend, ripped out of his life.

The deprivation was agonizing, and the utter helplessness he felt was almost as bad. What should he do now? Donate money to the American Cancer Society? Get himself sworn in as a deputy sheriff and go stamp out crime in the streets? It was a little too late to help Carole and Link.

Sitting under the umbrella, he twirled his gin and tonic and gazed at the kingfisher blue of the swimming pool. Link's daughter Pearl would be showing up any minute now. He hoped she wasn't coming over for a mutual sob session, but he couldn't think of any other reason for her wanting to drop in. As for himself, he was long since sobbed out and wrung dry, but he had loved Link and he loved Pearl and couldn't very well put her off when she telephoned. Ah, well, if misery loves company, so be it.

The pool motor clicked on and the pump roiled the blue surface. It was far past the time when he should have turned the pool heater on again, but he knew he wouldn't, not just for himself. He couldn't bear to swim alone now; it would only remind him of how he and Carole used to dive in together, naked, at night, with the underwater light turning the pool into a liquid blue topaz, and then they'd go inside . . .

He clenched his jaw and rubbed the bullet scar on his cheek as if to erase the memory. He looked instead at the flowers and greenery along the wall on the other side of the pool. Beyond the wall, the rest of his property was something of a waste. The ground rose steeply to the top of a knoll. Pine trees stood on the knoll, thrusting up from a green ground cover of Algerian ivy that prevented erosion. He must remember to turn on the sprinklers. The weather was getting hot.

The low-lying lobelias bloomed darkly blue at the edge of the pool deck, with flame-orange gazanias behind them, and then the blues and pinks of Carole's Canterbury bells and foxgloves and red gladiolas and ginger, all glowing against the jungle backdrop of the banana trees. Last year at this time she was among them with her yellow gloves and her sharp Swedish knife, cutting bouquets for the house. "Always use a knife," she explained to him, "never scissors, and they'll last longer. Scissors squash the stems."

This was the house he had had his eyes on for years, just east of the university on Sunset Boulevard. He never thought he would have the money to buy it, even if it came on the market, but both things happened. His father and mother left him a considerable sum. He saved money in the service. His book of war poems sold nicely and won a five-thousand-dollar literary prize. But most amazingly, although writing college textbooks is scarcely the road to riches, he had published a textbook and workbook for freshman English composition that unaccountably caught fire and took off like a rocket. Whether the reason was the excellence of the books, or lucky timing, or both, not even the publisher knew. But the royalties poured in and inflamed his colleagues with envy— renewed envy; it already rankled them that Cliff was a direct lineal descendant of the late-medieval Scottish poet William Dunbar. "See? Dreams do come true, Dunbar," said Fate, rolling his cigar to the side of his mouth. Dunbar's Fate looked like Telly Savalas. "Happy now?" Oh, sure.

The ship's bell clanged at the front of the house. The loud bell was Carole's idea, so she could hear it from the garden.

Cliff padded down the narrow sidewalk between the one-story Spanish house and the garage, and around to the front. Pearl stood by the bell in his deeply recessed doorway.

"Hello, Pearl. How are you?"

"Oh, there you are, Cliff! Hello!"

He kissed her cheek. She wore a short-sleeved white Mexican eyelet dress and held a white beaded clutch purse in both hands. He was relieved; this didn't look like mourning. In fact, aside from slightly puffy eyes from recent crying, Pearl looked pretty good. True, gravity had been pulling downward on the skin of her cheeks and neck for forty-odd years, but she was a nice-looking woman. "More beauty have I seen in one autumnal face . . ." Now, who was the poet who said that? Donne? He ought to be ashamed of himself, the certified expert on English literature.

"Come on out in back, Pearl. That's where the hooch is."

She laughed and followed him to the umbrella table.

"What can I fix you?"

"Whatever you're having."

"Gin and tonic with a lime."

"Ideal for a day in June."

" 'Then, if ever, come perfect days.' Sorry, Pearl. Excuse the graveyard humor."

"If you can stand it, I can."

"I'm glad you're here, Pearl. I'll feel less like an old Skid Row souse if I'm drinking with somebody."

"Oh, come on. You don't have your bottle in a paper bag."

"I threw the bag in the bushes when you rang the bell."

There was a pause, signifying that they would both just as soon drop the lighthearted banter, but neither one was sure what tone to adopt next. To bridge the gap, Cliff fixed his eyes on the glass and frowned as he poured. He wondered what was on Pearl's mind and whether he should ask, but Pearl gave the conversational ball another spin.

"Have you actually handed in your resignation now?"

Rattle of ice cubes. "Yep."

"You'll be a terrific loss to them. They're damn fools to lose someone of your caliber."

"I thought so, too, a few months ago. Now I'm not so sure."

"How so?"

"Oh, the English faculty irritated the hell out of me, true, but as I look back on it, I think I took too much pleasure rubbing their fur the wrong way."

Pearl laughed. "Exactly the right metaphor. Dad always referred to them as 'that bunch of goddamn pussycats.' "

"Link was too partisan for my side. They've got some good people."

"But those hypocrites running the department! Like firing that poor young assistant professor because he's gay, and pretending it was because he didn't publish enough in the *PMLA* or whatever. Honestly!"

"Yes, that was pretty bad. And standing up for him cost me the last three Brownie points I had. But listen, Pearl—I appreciate your loyalty, but I've decided I'm not really such a nice guy after all. I've got a temper. I can get mean and malicious, I enjoy making an issue over trivia because I enjoy a good fight, and I keep succumbing to the temptation to play Hemingway-*macho* among the pussycats."

"Among the pussycats, how can you avoid it? Holding a Silver Star and a Purple Heart from Vietnam. I'll bet they hated that."

"They did; but they could pooh-pooh it because Vietnam fell way below the standards of the liberal-arts types."

"It fell below mine, too."

"And mine—but I wasn't about to admit that to them. I just told 'em I was serving my country, which I was, and besides, I had to go because I was a reserve officer and I got called up."

"What did they say to that?"

"They thought I should have gone to jail like Thoreau."

"Piffle."

"Piffle, indeed."

"Who'll they get to teach medievalism in the fall?"

"I hear they're trying to import a big name from the East—maybe Higgins from Princeton, or Najarian from Yale."

"What do you think that'll mean for the medieval library in Special Collections?"

"I have no idea."

"According to Dad, you practically created the medieval collection single-handed."

"Wrong. *He* created it. All I did was make the suggestion. I pointed out how weak our holdings were and gave him advice on acquisitions. He took it from there, bless him, and was he ever a fireball! For starters, he even wangled a fourteenth-century manuscript of the *Romance of the Rose* out of the Bibliothèque Nationale in Paris."

"I know. He was really proud of that."

"So the university started to attract more medieval scholars, and all because of Link."

"You had a part in it. 'And now,' said Dad, 'just as we're developing a west-of-the-Mississippi reputation, the son-of-a-bitch quits!' "

"That's great! I can just hear old Link saying that!"

"He was all broken up about the school losing you."

"I was all broken up over losing Link."

Another long pause, marked by agitated ice-rattling.

"Which brings me to why I'm here," said Pearl.

"You don't mean to comfort *me*?"

"No. I want to ask you a favor—a pretty big favor."

"Your wish is my command."

"Don't be hasty. You haven't heard what it is."

"Okay."

"I want you to play detective."

"Oh? In what way?"

"I want to know who killed him. I want to see them caught. I want them to pay."

"Well, so do I, Pearl. But surely you're not suggesting that *I* look into the case?"

"I am. Nobody else is doing anything about it."

"That's crazy, Pearl! Hell, I'm no detective!"

"In a way you are. Your research makes you a literary detective. You've got the right kind of brains."

"Maybe. But there's a gigantic difference between analyzing Chaucer's *Legend of Good Women* and tracking down a murderer."

"I know. But who else can I turn to? I can't afford private detectives at two hundred dollars a day. Not on a computer programmer's pay."

Cliff sipped his drink, stalling for time, and looked blankly out into the garden. This was extremely awkward. He would have preferred a sob session.

"Pearl, dear, wait a minute. You're going way overboard. Nothing would please me more than running down those two thugs. I can't tell you how many times I've fantasized catching them and tearing them limb from bloody limb. But this is just wishful thinking. I know how frustrated you must feel and I feel the same way, but it's only been two weeks. Give the police a chance."

"Almost three weeks."

"All right, three. Have you pressured the police?"

"Yes, but they don't pressure. Oh, they're nice about it, they tell me the case is still on their open file, but they also say they've done all they can 'at this point in time.' They aren't encouraging. At least they're honest, though. Lieutenant Puterbaugh said that something like ninety percent of these cases are solved within twenty-four hours, usually by the cop on the beat talking to eyewitnesses and relatives. Cases that go beyond forty-eight hours usually stay unsolved."

"Well, if they can't solve it, what makes you think I could?"

"You're smarter than they are."

"Come on now, Pearl. That's like telling me I can build a better house than a carpenter because I've got a Ph.D."

"Let's say you can give it more thought, then. I think the police have quietly written it off. It would be different if Dad had been a movie star or a city councilman, but a librarian? I think they're just sitting back and hoping to catch the murderers in some new crime."

"Which they probably will. You can see the police's problem. A couple of unknown punks wandering the streets looking for somebody to rob . . ."

"They weren't wandering the streets. They were waiting for him in his apartment building's garage."

"Amounts to the same thing. And they didn't leave any handy clues behind—no strange leather buttons or prescription eyeglasses or garments with dry cleaner's numbers."

"No," she said bitterly, "all they left was a dead librarian with a rare book in his hand. And what's one librarian more or less? I honestly believe people cared more about the *Bay Psalm Book* than they did about Dad."

"That certainly doesn't apply to me. I'd give everything I own if it would bring him back—my house, everything."

"I know you mean that, and it's why I'm turning to you. I'd rather have you investigate the case, but if you don't want to, could you loan me some money? Four thousand dollars would buy twenty days from a private detective. I could pay you back when Dad's estate is settled."

"Pearl, you're making me feel terrible! Of course, I *want* to!"

"Then you'll do it?"

"That isn't what I meant."

He looked at her puffy eyes, now lit up with hope, and he couldn't bear it.

"Oh, Pearl, Pearl . . . I'll go this far. I'll take a preliminary look *at* the case, at least to the extent of seeing whether there's any point in my trying to pursue it."

"I'll settle for that. And I'll pay your expenses."

"No, you won't! I'll do it for Link—and you—and myself. I owe your father a lot more than money. He was my father too, in a way."

"You'd be surprised how much confidence I have in you."

"And you'd be surprised how little I have. When you asked me to 'play detective,' you couldn't have chosen better words. That's just what I'll be doing, playing at it. And the minute I see I'm in over my head I'm going to back out, and we'll just have to leave it to the police."

"Fair enough."

"Okay. Do you think it would do any good if I looked at the police file—providing they'd let me see it?"

"None at all. I've seen the file, and they don't know any more than what was in the newspapers."

"Wonderful. All right, then, I'll start with the newspapers."

"God bless you, Cliff! And good hunting!"

Two

"Good hunting," she says, thought Cliff, switching on his desk lamp. This mission was ridiculous and rather sad. It made him feel like one of those crazy scholars who insist that Shakespeare couldn't have written plays like *Hamlet* or *The Merchant of Venice* because he never went to college and spend years trying to force the evidence to fit Christopher Marlowe or Francis Bacon.

The clipping from the *Times* still lay in his top desk drawer. He took out the clipping and read it once again.

"THUGS KILL FOR $14, MISS A FORTUNE."

Very funny. The joke was on them.

> May 28. Lincoln Schofield, 62, Curator of Special Collections at the Los Angeles University Library, was fatally stabbed last night in the garage of his apartment building at 1624 Casuarina Avenue, Westwood, the apparent victim of a robbery duo. Found near the body was Schofield's wallet, from which $14 was reportedly missing. Unknown to the robbers was the fact that Schofield was carrying, in his right hand, a copy of the rare *Bay Psalm Book*, the first book printed in the American colonies, valued at nearly $300,000. The book, one of only eleven known existing copies, was donated to the library last December by Perry Winthrop, candidate for governor in the forthcoming November election.

> The body was discovered by a neighbor, Floretta

Bishop, who was walking her dog nearby at 9:00 P.M., the approximate time of the murder. She reported seeing two black men emerge hurriedly from the garage and proceed rapidly past her, walking northward toward Wilshire Boulevard. She thought little of it at the time but peered into the garage as she reached it with her dog, saw Schofield's body, and notified the police from the telephone of a tenant in Schofield's apartment building.

Bishop reported seeing the two suspects clearly as they passed her at the intersection of Casuarina and Oleander. One was about six feet, two inches tall, one hundred fifty pounds, medium brown in complexion, wearing a floppy-sleeved white nylon shirt, a beige vest, and bell-bottomed slacks with rows of brass buttons along triangular slashes in the cuffs. His companion was about five feet six, a hundred eighty pounds, very dark-complexioned, with a bushy Afro hair style, blue jeans, and a white T-shirt bearing the inscription "Phuque You." Both were in their early twenties. An all-points bulletin has been issued for their apprehension.

A paper bag containing stationery supplies and a cash-register receipt, found near the body, led investigators to the Paper Place, a stationery store in Westwood, where Schofield made purchases amounting to $6.00 at about 8:40 P.M. A clerk recalled his saying jokingly, "There goes my last twenty. I'll have to go home and print up some more if I want to join the Pyramid Club tonight." This led police to deduce that Schofield had only $14 in his wallet when he was accosted.

[Terrific, thought Dunbar. The tradition of Nero Wolfe and Albert Campion is not dead.]

University officials were at a loss to explain why

Schofield had the *Bay Psalm Book* in his possession but were relieved, as was Winthrop, the donor, that the near-priceless volume is again safe under lock and key in Special Collections.

Schofield, a widower, had been curator of Special Collections for the past twenty years, prior to which he worked for the Folger Library in Washington, D.C., famed for its collection of Shakespeare folios and quartos. He is survived by his daughter, Mrs. Pearl Humphrey, a senior programmer for Information Science Associates, a research firm in Santa Monica.

Dunbar set the clipping aside, knowing no more than when he had first read it, which was nothing. If only he were Hercule Poirot, he reflected ruefully, he could sit back and put his little gray cells to work and solve the problem with a brilliant flash of deduction, or at least seize on a glaring clue that everyone had overlooked. His little gray cells merely lay in his skull like oatmeal, however. Nor did he see any clues at all, large or small. In such a case, then, where would your obscure, plodding, workaday private eye begin? The answer to that was easy enough, there being only one possibility.

He got out the Western Section of the Pacific Telephone Directory and copied Floretta Bishop's phone number and address into his pocket notebook. He picked up the phone and started to punch the buttons, but paused and replaced the receiver. It was too easy for people to say no over the telephone, and if she said no he'd feel boorish and intrusive if he then showed up anyway and pounded on her door. Better pound on her door first.

But what then? No doubt, if she let him in at all, she'd repeat the details that appeared in the newspaper, politely show him out, and leave him standing in the foyer sucking his thumb like the village idiot. But one never knows, and she lived only a mile or so away, on Wilkinson.

He backed his orange Porsche out of the garage—the English faculty fined him ten more Brownie points when he bought that car—down the gravel driveway and cautiously out onto Sunset Boulevard, cutting in as close to the curb as possible and gunning forward as fast as possible. The one drawback to his dream house was its being on a sharp curve, around which careened the cream of the Los Angeles Wild Drivers' Association. Get careless for one short interlude and a roaring rear-ender could punt him clear over the campus and into the Medical Center parking lot.

Floretta Bishop lived in a condominium on one of the pleasant, narrow, quiet, tree-shaded streets south of Wilshire. Cliff got out of his car and paused to admire the place. Very modern. Façade all vertical redwood planks, dark glass, black wrought iron, shiny glabrous leaves of camellia, gardenia, magnolia, and fiery red splashes of hibiscus blooms. Floretta's condominium must have cost her three or four hundred thousand, depending on when she bought it. No pauper, Floretta.

She lived on the ground floor, looking out on the leafy street. Cliff rang the doorbell, setting off a frenzy of barking from a small dog inside. "Berf! Berf! Ber-er-er-berf! Berf-berf!" A square iron peephole opened in the heavy wooden door, and a glittering black eye scrutinized him.

"Who is it?"

"I'm Dr. Clifford Dunbar from the university, Mrs. Bishop. I'm a friend of Lincoln Schofield, the murdered man you discovered."

"What do you want?"

"Just to ask you a few questions about it, if I may."

"Well . . . all right."

The eye disappeared and Cliff heard the sound of a solid deadbolt lock being slid back and of a heavy chain being unhooked. No patsy either, Floretta.

The door opened and he found himself facing a woman who reminded him of the drawing of the Gorgon Medusa in *Bul-*

finch's Mythology. Not that Floretta looked hideous or had snaky hair; on the contrary, she was beautifully dressed, and her face would have been all right if the corners of her mouth curved upward instead of sharply downward—that and those two jet-black eyes set in a heavily powdered face. Floretta appeared to be about sixty striving to look forty. Her chances would have been better had she melted off thirty pounds or so of pudge.

"I was just going out. But come in. Sit down. Excuse me. I'll put my hat back on the block."

Her hat was of the flower-pot type, encircled with velvet pansies and nasturtiums and a dotted veil. Her brief disappearance allowed Cliff a quick examination of the living room. Outside, the building was late twentieth century, but it was mostly eighteenth century in here: a blue-and white-striped empire divan behind a drum coffee table. Queen Anne chairs with gracefully curving legs, big honey-and-blue Kirman Shah rug, a convex mirror framed in gold ormolu, competent English landscapes by unknown English painters depicting cows, fields, thatched-roof cottages, hollyhocks, and milkmaids. All very nice, but the room looked as if it had come as a package straight fom Barker Brothers. The exception was a large oil painting of a nude that hung above the Georgian fireplace. The pose and execution were much like Manet's *Olympe*—very good indeed, up to a point—or, rather, two points, for the artist abandoned Impressionism when he came to the model's breasts, which he rendered with almost *trompe l'oeil* realism. The creamy brushstrokes circled about them lovingly; a faint blue tracery of veins appeared; the two pink aureoles were tipped with crinkled pink nipples. Blue shadows beneath the breasts seemed to thrust them forward toward the viewer, inviting a naughty nip or two.

It was not the only incongruity in the room. Cliff noted that not a single photograph, knickknack, souvenir, postcard, or artsy-craftsy piece revealed that a human being with a personal life lived here, unless one counted the little Chinese pagoda in the corner with the name "Yu Shan" inscribed over the door. Yu Shan, the peke, had retreated to it and lay on a tasseled velvet cushion inside, glowering out at him suspiciously with bulging eyeballs.

When Floretta reappeared, they sat down facing each other on two of the harp-backed Queen Anne chairs. Yu Shan promptly leaped into her lap.

"Now. What can I tell you that you haven't already read in the newspapers?" She scratched Yu Shan's right ear.

"Probably nothing at all, Mrs. Bishop. It is 'Mrs.'? I'm really sorry to bother you, but I promised Lincoln's daughter that I'd try to find out any details that may have been overlooked."

"There aren't any. The police questioned me thoroughly." She patted her hair, jet black like her eyes and pulled back into a bun so tight that a wrinkle on her forehead didn't have a chance.

"I'm sure they did, but since you were the first one to stumble on the murder scene, I thought—"

"It was a very unpleasant experience."

"Of course. And you got a clear look at the killers?"

"I saw them from the corner of Casuarina and Oleander, coming out of the garage. They walked right past me under the streetlight. Two young coloreds."

Cliff's eyebrows went up.

"You're sure they were—black?"

"One of them was. Black as the ace of spades. The other one was a sort of mild-chocolate brown. Mulatto."

Floretta missed Cliff's tactful correction, but then she belonged to an older generation. He hadn't heard the word "mulatto" in years. He shrugged it off.

"They couldn't have been whites—disguised with burnt cork, for instance?"

"I know a colored when I see one."

"I suppose so; and one of them sported an Afro, I understand."

"The tall one."

"Didn't the way they were dressed strike you as odd?"

"No. Coloreds go for all sorts of outrageous getups, especially the men."

"But wouldn't you think two black men on a crime spree would have better sense than to roam an upper-class white neighborhood dressed like Laurel and Hardy at a costume ball? You'd think they went out of their way to make themselves conspicuous. After all, bell-bottomed slacks and an obscene T-shirt! And why were they on foot? Why didn't they have a getaway car nearby?"

"My dear young man, don't ask me how their minds work. I don't care what people say, they're still primitives. Do you know I have seen Negro men with craps inset in gold in their two front teeth? A five and a two, for Christ's sake! When I was in business I wouldn't have one of them on the place."

"What business were you in?"

"I was an entertainment manager. I'm not surprised they used knives on poor Mr. Schofield. Negroes are very fond of cutlery, you know."

A geyser of rage spouted inside Cliff and, finding no outlet, attempted to erupt through his eyeballs.

The green jungle and the muddy brown stream flashed into his mind yet again. The water felt good as he sloshed through it, leading the reconnaissance patrol. As he stumbled out of the shallow water on the other bank, the Cong sniper got him. The bullet hit just to the right of his right eyebrow, plowed downward through his cheek, exited, then plowed through the skin and muscle of his right shoulder. He fell face downward in the water. The sniper fired again and missed. Sergeant Philip Fixico, black as the ace of spades, plunged into the stream under fire and dragged him out. As they reached the safety of the jungle fringe, Fixico took a slug at the upper end of his left femur, shattering the joint, with the result that Fixico was walking around Hollywood today with a silver ball-joint inserted in the socket of his pelvis.

Too bad Mrs. Bishop couldn't see it; it would make a nice

addition to her story about the gold craps in the teeth. But then again, Fixico was disappointing; he didn't carry a knife or a razor, not really needing one in his work as a Hollywood agent for black actors and actresses.

It cost him, but Cliff fought back the storm behind his eyeballs. He had to, if he wanted to get information from Floretta Bishop instead of a bitter brouhaha that would end with his ass out on the sidewalk. He had Pearl to think of, and Link.

Cliff rubbed the bullet scar and felt the bristles down in the crease that made shaving difficult.

"I'm afraid you and I differ strongly about black people, Mrs. Bishop, partly because one of them saved my life once."

"I suppose that would make a difference."

"Yes. But let's press on with the sleuthing. What exactly did you see when you went into Link's garage?"

"Link's? Oh, you mean Lincoln Schofield. Well—what I told the police. He was lying face down in a pool of blood. The garage light was out. The cops said somebody may have unscrewed the bulb or else it just came loose. But I saw his empty wallet lying there and he had a book in his hand. That's all."

"The bulb was unscrewed? That suggests that the killers were waiting for him—maybe knew he was coming."

"I doubt it. They were probably ready to jump the first tenant who showed up."

"Of course. Probably you're right. Then what did you do?"

"I hurried up the steps and phoned the police from a woman's apartment."

"Do you remember whose it was?"

"A little old lady. I never caught her name."

"Do you remember the apartment number?"

"No. I tried two or three doors before I found someone at home."

"What did you do then?"

"I went back down and stayed with the body till the police showed up. To make sure nobody touched anything—like in the movies. And that's it. That's all I know."

"Exactly what was in the papers."

"Yes. Sorry."

She took a walnut cream from a candy box on the dropleaf table to her left and held it out to Yu Shan. The dog snorted and snapped it up, chewing it at one corner of his mouth.

"Isn't that bad for his teeth?"

"Sure it is. But Yu Shan and I would both rather go first class and die young than live forever on dry kibble. And what do you care, anyway?"

"I don't. Just making conversation."

"In that case, you will excuse me now. I have errands."

"Uh—only one thing, Mrs. Bishop. About those two men—the short, fat one and the tall one with the Afro?"

"Yes?"

"The tall one had the Afro?"

"Sure. Why?"

"You were quoted in the paper as saying it was the short one."

"Oh!" For a moment she resembled a deer who has heard a twig snap in the forest. "Well, it was the short one. I wasn't thinking. And now you *must* excuse me, Dr. Dunbar."

"Of course, and thank you very much for your trouble."

He drove the three short blocks to Link's apartment building on Casuarina.

"You certainly learned a lot, didn't you, Sherlock?" he said to himself. "Caught her in a contradiction, too, that doesn't make a damn one way or the other. A real pro!"

He walked into the garage and looked at the spot where they had found Link. He saw nothing but a few faded rusty splotches resembling drippings from a leaky radiator. Perhaps, engrained in the concrete, were a few shiveled corpuscles, all that remained above the earth of his old friend. Being there, looking down at the floor where Link had lain, where the police had no doubt outlined him in chalk, made Cliff angry.

The waste! That word, used as a verb so loosely and wrongly in Vietnam, fit this senseless murder truly and miserably. Fourteen dollars! His muscles tightened. He resolved to shape up, come alert, bend his mind fully to this problem and not make a lazy dogtrot through it just to show Pearl he had "tried."

He ran up the steps to the first-floor hallway. An unsealed envelope inscribed "Mark" was scotch-taped to the door of apartment 101. As a sleuth, Cliff felt entitled to have a look at it. He took a folded note from the envelope. "Mark," it read, "you should know me well enough by now to realize that when I say no I mean *no!*" The last "no" was underlined four times. "You will kindly put your key in this envelope, shove it under the door, and go resume your meaningful relationship with Shannon. I am vindictive enough to hope you marry each other. Good-bye. Heidi."

"Ah, Heidi," thought Cliff, smiling as he replaced the note, "Chaucer should have known about you when he was ordered to write 'a glorious legende of goode women and telle of false men—like Mark—that hem bytraien.' "

No one answered the bell in 102. A card on the door of 103 identified the occupant as Mrs. Goldina Fuller. He heard her footsteps approaching after he rang the bell, and he quickly stood so she would see mostly the left side of his face when she peered through the fisheye lens in her door. If this was Floretta Bishop's little old lady, it wouldn't do for her to see a stand-in for Paul Muni in *Scarface*. He might never get in.

She looked him over carefully before she opened up.

"You understand, Dr. Dunbar, I've been jumpy as a cat ever since that awful incident in the garage."

"I don't blame you at all, ma'am."

"Are you a detective?"

"No, just a friend of the murdered man."

"That's so terrible, losing a friend that way! And he was such a nice man. I didn't really know Mr. Schofield, but he was always very cordial to me."

"He was a prince, and I miss him so much my stomach hurts."

"Sit down, Dr. Dunbar. I just fixed some iced tea. Let me pour you a glass."

"Why, thank you."

Mrs. Fuller reminded him of his grandmother, small and wiry and tough, but with kind brown eyes. The apartment smelled pleasantly of roses, and cotton hot from ironing, and Jergens lotion, and what he was sure must be the same Cuticura salve his grandmother used.

She returned from the kitchen with a tray bearing a frosty pitcher of dark tea and ice cubes and a dozen slices of lemon and two tall glasses—Depression glass, he noted. She handed him his glass, sat down, and took her own.

"Now, sire! You may commence your interrogation!"

"Very well, madam," he said, laughing, "I ask you to recall the night of May 28 . . . Good heavens!"

"What's the matter?"

"Mrs. Fuller, this iced tea is magnificent! I've never tasted anything like it!"

"Oh, pshaw, it isn't anything. Of course, it's rare out here. Have you ever been in Pinckneyville, Illinois?"

"Afraid I haven't."

"It's only about thirty miles north of Carbondale. You draw a line through Pinckneyville from east to west—Virginia to Kansas—and only people south of that line know how to make iced tea. You have to make it double strength because the ice will dilute it, and let it set a while, and then add sugar and lemons and ice."

"I assure you I'm going to remember that."

"Mr. Fuller used to drink it by the gallon, winter and summer. Of course, the winters out here aren't as cold, but nevertheless I used to say to him, 'Abe, you're running a good thing into the ground. You're going to iced-tea yourself to death one of these days, and I know whereof I speak!' And he'd just grin and say, 'Want me to switch to gin, Goldie?' And I'd say, 'No, but there's so much tannin in that tea you're going to wind up with a stomach like an alligator suitcase,' and he'd just laugh and fill his glass again. Well, I was wrong. He was president of his bag and twine company, and he worked right up to the day he died of a heart attack in his office at the age of seventy."

"How long has he been gone?"

"Six years now."

"I lost my wife last fall."

"Oh, *dear*, oh, dear! How *awful*! How old was she?"

"Twenty-eight."

"How frightful! And here I was, feeling sorry for myself, and I have forty years of a happy marriage to look back on! Well, at least you're young and you can marry again."

"Perhaps, if I can ever find another Carole—or a Goldina Fuller."

"Is that a proposal, Dr. Dunbar?"

"Well, I don't want to rush you."

For a pleasant while, they traded reminiscences—she of southern Illinois and moving to California to set up in bag and twine, he of his grasshopper youth jumping from one Army post to another in the mainland United States, Hawaii, and Germany, following his father, a lieutenant colonel in the infantry. Good schools, bad schools, two years here, two years there. Cliff virtually educated himself because of his penchant for reading everything he could get his hands on, and he also ended up speaking fluent German and French.

The afternoon sun moved behind the jacaranda tree outside and ignited a hundred clustered blossoms into lavender lanterns.

"Well, back to business, reluctantly," said Cliff. "Mrs. Bishop telephoned the police from your apartment?"

"Yes, she rang my bell a little after nine and said there'd

been a murder in the garage and could she use my phone to call the police. Of course I let her."

"How did she act? Pretty upset, I suppose."

"Cool as a cucumber. You'd have thought she was calling a cab. I was the one who was upset."

"I should imagine."

"My heart was thumping lickety-split, but she just hung up and said thank you like she'd done me a favor coming in, and sashayed out like she was the Queen of Sheba."

"I've talked to her and she struck me the same way."

"If the truth be known, it wouldn't surprise me if she used to be a chippie, with her eyelids painted green as june bugs."

"Chippie?"

"A woman of ill fame. But I shouldn't speak bad of her just because I didn't like her. 'Judge not, that ye be not judged,' as it says in Scripture."

"You didn't hear anything yourself that night?"

"No, not a thing."

"Did you go down to the garage?"

"Mercy, no! I locked my door and stayed put."

"Did the police talk to you?"

"Yes, but I couldn't tell them anything. Mrs. Bishop gave them an earful, of course."

"Have there been any other incidents like that in the neighborhood that you know of?"

"Oh, no, there's very little crime around here, unless you count boys shooting out streetlights and stealing hubcaps. And the girl down in 101 had her bicycle stolen. Could I pour you some more iced tea?"

"No, thanks, I'd better be moving along. I much appreciate your talking to me, Mrs. Fuller."

"Why, it's been a pleasure. It's been a long time since I've entertained a young man in my apartment—and with the door closed!"

She laughed as roguishly as a schoolgirl and showed him to the door.

"If I think of more questions, may I call on you again?"

"Of course."

"And I'm going to make myself some iced tea like that. If I fail, I may call you for further instructions."

"You're welcome any time."

Cliff paused in the open doorway. "Mrs. Fuller—when I came in here I was feeling pretty depressed. I want you to know that you've shored up my faith in humanity."

He leaned over and gave her a quick kiss on the cheek.

"Pshaw! Look out, young man, or you won't escape so easily next time!"

"Good-bye, Mrs. Fuller."

She closed the door smiling.

Cliff skipped down the steps with a lighter heart, although he hadn't learned a thing except that there are still good people in the world.

Standing on the front sidewalk, he looked northward up Casuarina. The street curved gracefully upward on a slope, intersected Oleander, and went on toward Wilshire. It was a clean street, and leafy. At the intersection of Casuarina and Oleander, on the other side, a slender lamppost arched over the pavement, no doubt the one under which Mrs. Bishop saw her two "coloreds." From there she'd have an oblique but clear angle of vision toward the garage opening where he stood. He walked over to the spot.

Still holding his "detective notebook" in his hand, he looked up at the streetlight, suddenly feeling idiotic for doing it, as if it were going to tell him anything.

"Are you the insurance adjuster? It's been replaced."

Cliff turned around to see a woman who had popped up from some low shrubbery on the other side of a white picket fence. She wore gardening gloves and held a trowel in her hand. She had a round, red, cheerful face and a knobby nose, sunburned at the tip.

"Oh, hello. No, I'm not. Just looking around."

"Darn! What on earth takes them so long?"

"Who?"

"Insurance companies. They love to rake it in, but oh, boy, do they hate to pay out! Howsomever, you can't be interested in my little troubles."

"On the contrary, I'm all ears."

"I fail to see why, unless you're that kid's father. I hope you are."

"What kid?"

She pointed with her trowel. "That kid over there eating the snow cone. He's the one wot done it."

A fat boy in T-shirt and tennis shoes sat on the curb over on Oleander, his mouth pressed into a paper cone full of crushed ice, presumably lime and of a violent green unknown in nature. He lowered the cone, revealing a brilliant moustache and goatee.

" 'And then I hit upon a plan to dye my whiskers green,' " said Cliff.

The woman waggled her trowel. " 'But always use so large a fan that they could not be seen.' "

They laughed together. Cliff denied paternity of the fat boy and introduced himself.

"And I'm Melinda Mendenhall."

"And wot was it he done?" asked Cliff.

"Shot out the streetlight, 'e did. Oh, I can't prove it, but he's the only kid around here with a pellet gun. When that glass broke and fell—well, have you any idea how thick those glass covers are? About a quarter of an inch. One chunk cracked my windshield—my VW Rabbit was parked right underneath—and the rest of it crashed on the roof and made about six deep dents. Brand-new car. I reported it to the insurance company, and I haven't heard from them since. Ergo, my remark to you when you showed up."

"No, as a matter of fact, Mrs. Mendenhall, just on my own I'm looking into the murder of Lincoln Schofield, the man who was killed down the street. He was a good friend."

"What a frightful thing that was! I'm so sorry! Both things happened the same evening, you know."

"What things?"

"The murder and the streetlight."

His interest quickened. "Really? Was the streetlight shot out before or after the murder?"

"Easily two hours before."

"That's very curious. The woman who saw the two killers come out of the garage said she was standing on this spot when they hurried past her. She said she got a good look at them under the light."

"Then she's either lying or embroidering—unless she meant that streetlight over there."

Some fifty feet past the fat boy, to the west, another lamp-post arched among the trees over Oleander.

"No," said Cliff. "From there she could see your house, but she couldn't see around the corner to that garage."

"Could she have meant the streetlight down *below*, at Casuarina and Tamarind?"

"No, she distinctly said Oleander."

"Then I suggest you have another word with her. That's a pretty peculiar story."

"Indeed. Well, thanks very much, Mrs. Mendenhall. You've given me my first clue."

"Go get 'em, Philo."

He returned to his car and hurried back to Floretta Bishop's apartment, but she was gone. Frustrated, he sat in the Porsche and wondered what to do next. Go have a beer? The afternoon was hot. Wait here until Floretta came back? Too boring. Nothing in the car to read. Go buy a book and sit in the car and read it? Dumb. Go home and call her later? Maybe.

His excitement evaporated. Where was this going to get him, anyway? All right, Floretta was either lying or confused or embroidering. But why would she lie? Only if she knew the killers, and that idea was preposterous. If she knew the killers, she would hardly drag Yu Shan over to Casuarina to see how the boys were doing. Confused? Doubtful. She had a mind like a pocket calculator. Embroidering was much more likely—a case of the witness who, once in the limelight, doesn't want to appear wishywashy and uncertain and therefore nails down every detail with twice the certainty the witness actually feels. All Mrs. Bishop had to say was, "Look—streelight or no streetlight, I saw them clearly and that's that," and his piddling clue would evaporate.

In short, he was nowhere. Again—what to do next? "Nothing," answered the other voice in his inner dialog. "Go home and call Pearl and tell her to leave it to the police, and start thinking about what you're going to do with your own future."

The idea made his stomach writhe. What *was* he going to do with his life? If he so chose, of course, he could merely sit and slowly rot all by himself in the garden of his dream house. He had enough money to do it. The house, which he had bought for two hundred thousand, had shot up to a value of one million in the ridiculous Southern California market, and his liquid assets totaled about half a million. Half a million, even at a feeble 10 percent, and he could alternately work *London Times* crossword puzzles and read through the complete works of Dickens until his beard smothered him.

He wasn't ready for that yet. He returned gratefully to the case of Lincoln Schofield. One curious question remained about Link. Obviously it had nothing to do with his murder, but what was he doing larking about Westwood that night with a well-nigh priceless book in his hand—one that he had no business removing from the library in the first place?

To be sure, it was characteristic of the old son-of-a-gun that he didn't really give a damn about the *Bay Psalm Book*. To Link, books were objects that either did or did not possess intrinsic interest or beauty. The Gutenberg Bible, for instance, aside from its historical importance, was a beautiful specimen of the printer's art. The pamphletlike "parts" in which *Pickwick Papers* first appeared were a fanfare of trumpets announcing the arrival of a major new writer. Link did not hold any book in reverential awe merely because it was worth a great deal of money—an attitude that had plainly irritated Perry Winthrop at the presentation ceremony for the *Bay Psalm Book*. Link was sufficiently gracious and appreciative, but Winthrop wanted him bowled over, agog, ebullient, and expansive in the publicity photos. Instead, Link favored the camera with a tolerant half smile and a thumb hooked into a vest pocket.

Over glasses of punch after the ceremony, Link had passed judgment on the book to Cliff. "First book printed in the American colonies. Calloo, callay, oh, frabjous day. But what can you do with it? Look at the bloody book: It's ugly, and it's absolutely unreadable! So you take one look at it, riffle the pages, and say, 'Yep, that's the *Bay Psalm Book*, all right,' and you stick it on the shelf and never look at it again."

"Come on, Link," replied Cliff, laughing. "At least the Preface tells us more about how seriously the Puritans took their religion—especially that curious insistence of theirs that the Psalms actually had to be sung out loud."

"And having said that, you've said it all. No, the book stinks, and it seems to have set a gawky and dismal tone that ran through American literature for the next two hundred years. My old dad used to snort and protest that when *he* went to college they didn't even bother to *teach* American literature!"

Given such an attitude, what had Link been doing with the book that night? He certainly wasn't bringing it home for bedtime reading. On the grounds that your supersleuth overlooks nothing, Cliff started his motor and headed for the university.

THREE

*H*e left his Porsche in a parking building and felt a sharp twinge of regret, in spite of himself, that his faculty sticker would expire in a scant three weeks and thenceforth he would have to make sure he had quarters in his pocket to operate the parking gate. It would mark a turning point in his life. Even though he had resigned, he felt as if he had been expelled from the company of the blessed. He had been banished, and his enemies would exult.

He made his way through the coral trees around Matthews Hall and emerged on the quad. The rosy-orange brick of the buildings glowed in the afternoon sunlight. Facing him was the mass of the central university library, straining to keep its two million books from bursting through the walls. He had spent many an hour down in its dark stacks, doing research on unbelievably recondite subjects—almost as bad as Aldous Huxley's "Certain Aspects of a Merovingian Belt Buckle" but not quite—until he'd gone stir-crazy. Then he'd rush home, grab his fly rod and fishing vest, and scorch the road up to the San Gabriel River, where the rippling water, the wind in the big-cone spruce trees, and the silver flash of rainbow trout blew the book dust off his cerebellum. He released all the trout he caught. He knew he'd be needing them again.

Cliff crossed the quad and mounted the wide stone steps into the library. Turning right, he went down to Special Collections at the end of the hall. He hesitated at the door, not wanting to go in and see the place without Link there, high up on a library ladder or chewing out some frightened student researcher for laying an open book face down on a table. Well, at least Akira Yonenaka would be there. He pushed the door open and went in.

It was a long room with high, glass-fronted, locked bookcases around the walls, and rows of oak tables where a few graduate students hunched in intense concentration over rare books. The books were propped onto upright reading racks and were held open by dangling tubular bags made of velvet and filled with sand.

At Cliff's end of the room was a counter behind which stood Akira Yonenaka, Link's assistant, conducting business with a graduate student. Behind Akira were two doors leading into the librarians' offices.

On the counter in front of the student lay a typewriter-paper box from which Akira was extracting sheets one at a time, peering at them, and scowling. Cliff recognized what was going on and smiled. As the final stage in the long climb to the Ph.D. degree, the student was submitting the master copy of his doctoral dissertation for acceptance into the archives of Special Collections. This was by no means a mere formality. The standards were steel-rigid, and Link and Akira, if they had to be, were hanging judges. If the paper was not 100 percent rag, if the margins were too narrow, the erasures too numerous or too deep, the print too light, or the format incorrect, the student had to have the entire dissertation retyped and would not get his or her degree until it was accepted.

Akira arrived at the last sheet, held it up to the light, squinted, and said, "Okay." The student wiped his sleeved arm across his forehead and blurted, "Jesus Christ, really? Thank you, Mr. Yonenaka! Thanks very much!"

"Nice job," said Akira.

"Well—thanks again!" The young man hurried out before the samurai could have second thoughts.

"Still scaring 'em spitless, I see."

"Hey! Cliff! How the hell are you? Let me put this away and I'll be right with you."

Akira carefully replaced the dissertation in its box and put it on a shelf together with the photocopies the student had submitted.

"Come on back to the office."

Akira raised a hinged barrier, and Cliff passed through.

"Coffee time," said Akira. He poured two cups from a glass urn and they sat down in his office, full of toppling stacks of paper, books with tickets projecting from them like pink tongues, books crisscrossed with rubber bands, destined for the university bindery, and piles of correspondence.

"It's a good thing you don't smoke in all this paper, Akira."

"You said it. Cigarettes and matches? I'd be jumpy as the Scarecrow of Oz. Nobody can smoke around here anyway—it's bad for the books."

"You look busy."

"Man, I've been going crazy, trying to do Link's work and my own, plus cleaning out Link's office." He looked down at his cup. "Which has not exactly been a pleasure."

"No."

"Pearl's already taken eight cartons of his things home—books, pictures, diplomas, that bust of Shakespeare, stuff out of his desk, and we aren't through yet. But you know, he's still here and he always will be, even if they remove everything right down to his fingerprints on the doorknob. This library *is* Link. He created it, and the whole thing is a physical extension of the man."

There was a muffled choke in his voice as he said it, and his eyes misted.

"Damn!" he muttered. "I'm not supposed to do that." He looked up owlishly. "I'm Japanese, you know."

"Geez, Akira—I didn't know that."

"Oh, yes! You never noticed, hey? Same thing happened to my doctor. Son-of-a-bitch treated me for yellow jaundice for three years before he realized I'm Oriental."

Cliff laughed. "What do you think's going to happen around here?" he asked. Will you move into Link's slot?"

"Maybe. It's what I'd like. But there's talk that they may make me librarian for the new Asian Studies Center. Guess why."

"You're inscrutable?"

"Got it. How about you? What are you going to do with yourself?"

"I've no idea. Write, maybe, if I can work up the urge again. One thing I know: I've graded my last blue book. I love the students and I love the classroom, but I just can't take all the stuff that goes with it."

"That's pretty apparent. If you don't mind my saying so, you have a reputation as a fine teacher and all that, but you always gave me the impression of being a displaced person— sort of a misfit, like a Hell's Angel at a Christian Endeavor meeting."

"Thanks a lot."

"You know it as well as I do. You don't act like an English professor, and you don't talk like one—like, what did Mark Twain call it?—like a ten-dollar love offering. They get under my skin sometimes."

"They do tend to become sesquipedalian on occasion."

"But aside from a desire to bask in my charm, what brings you here this afternoon?"

"Pearl asked me to look into Link's murder. See if I could find out anything more."

"She did? I thought it was an open-and-shut case—mostly shut."

"That's the way it looks. Oh, I found a couple of feeble leads I want to follow up, but right now I'm curious about why Link had the *Bay Psalm Book* with him."

"The police asked me that, too, and it baffles me."

"Link didn't even like the book."

"I know. And he didn't like Perry Winthrop either."

"Who does?"

"So far, probably half a million California voters. Don't underestimate him. He's foxy as they come."

"He proved that," said Cliff, "donating the *Bay Psalm Book* to Special Collections—after all his talk in the past about lazy professors dragging down big salaries for teaching twelve hours a week, and the need to cut the fat out of the university budget."

"To say nothing of the bone and muscle."

"Anti-intellectual as they come. The whole university system was ranked against him. And then he neatly pulled the rug out from the whole gang with his new line about making us the Harvard of the West and giving us the *Bay Psalm Book*. He won a lot of hearts and minds."

"For which, let us not forget, he claimed a three-hundred-thousand-dollar tax deduction."

"Of course. Should he be punished for his generosity?"

"Perish the thought. Have you noticed he's started wearing a vest?"

"Father figure."

"Hmph. But back to business. Try to be a wily Oriental and speculate on why Link had the book with him."

"Well, let's see. He's worried about its authenticity, and he takes it over to Archer at the Huntington for another opinion."

"Possible, but doubtful. The two most distinguished bibliographers in the country have already certified it: C. T. Post at Harvard and Bradford Silliman at Stanford. Why bother with No. 3—good, but still No. 3?"

"All right, maybe he took it across the quad to show to Dr. Derrick's bibliography class in Matthews Hall and didn't want to bother coming back here to lock it up."

"Again, possible. Be easy to check. But Link would have made the class come here to look at it, don't you think?"

"I suppose. But he may have taken it to show *somebody*."

"But who?"

"There you have me. Pearl, maybe?"

"Not a chance."

"Then I give up. What do *you* think?"

"I think you're right; he took it to show somebody."

"But who?"

Cliff grinned. "There you have me."

"Good. Glad we have that settled."

"What time did you see him last that day, Akira?"

"About two o'clock. He took off early. And come to think of it, that's too late for Derrick's class, so that one's out. . . . But, hey! I'm forgetting something."

"What?"

"Link started some kind of letter or note to you the day before he was killed. Come on, I'll show you."

They went next door into Link's office, now a bare and forlorn room, with cartons scattered about and clean rectangles on the wall where framed pictures and diplomas had hung. From a box filled with loose papers, Akira extracted a sheet of stationery with four lines typed on it.

The note read: "May 27th. Cliff—Perry Winthrop has garnered many laurels these past few months, and has even donated one of them to LAU. You will pardon the pun, but the man flourishes like the green bay-tree. As of today, however, *timeo Danaos et dona ferentis*." And here the note broke off.

Cliff frowned. "The Latin means 'I fear Greeks bearing gifts.' What do you suppose he's talking about?"

"Beats me. Where's the Trojan horse?"

"He's referring to the *Bay Psalm Book*, of course, but I don't get the connection. It implies that Winthrop or his gifts are something to be feared. Has he been making more donations?"

"No, only the two last December. Along with the *Bay Psalm Book* he gave us a first edition of Henry Adams's *Mont-St.-Michel and Chartres*, the one sponsored by the American Institute of Architects."

"I know. I was here for the ceremony. Funny thing to toss in the Adams. Nice to have, but there's no comparison between the two for value."

"Made him appear a trifle more bookish, maybe. And it emphasized his old New England connections."

"There's that. Mind if I take this note with me?"

"It's addressed to you."

Cliff folded it and put it in his jacket. "Many thanks, Akira. Be seeing you."

"Right. It's time I locked up the joint and went home myself. Let me know how the sleuthing goes. We Japanese are big on revenge, you know."

"Sure thing. *Sayonara.*"

"*Arrivederci,* Dunbar-*san.*"

FOUR

Cliff was awakened at six the next morning by the green
and yellow of early sunlight filtering through the broad arching leaves of the banana trees outside his bedroom window.

His throat was dry and a little sore, from which he deduced
that he had been sleeping on his back again and snoring like a
bulldog. Poor Carole; three or four times a night, she used to
have to punch him and say, "Cliff! Turn over on your side!" It
always made her very cross, too, to have her sleep disturbed,
except when he'd mutter, "Okay, Sergeant"—which usually
got a laugh out of her. It was the only fault in him that truly
exasperated her, although right on the borderline was his
chronic athlete's foot, which he rubbed from between his toes
with a ferocious scowl.

"Once in a while, my dear," she used to say, "just once in a
while, I think they should have left you in the jungle, where
you'd feel right at home. I wish your students could see you
right now."

He lay there for a time in the king-sized bed, missing her,
then got up and padded into the kitchen to put on a pot of
coffee. A glass of cold grapefruit juice cured the sore throat.
The refrigerator was nearly empty. He'd have to go to the
market in Westwood Village—and soon, maybe today, if he
didn't want to take to eating in restaurants all the time. He
went back into the bedroom and ran through his Royal
Canadian Air Force exercises.

At six-thirty he sat down in the kitchen with a cup of coffee
and telephoned Pearl Humphrey.

"Hope I didn't wake you up."

"No, I'm up. I have to be at work at eight."

"That's terrible. I had to teach an eight-o'clock section on Shakespeare once. Can you imagine talking about King Lear going mad at eight in the morning?"

"Is that what time he went mad? He got an early start on the day, didn't he?"

"You're sounding cheerful."

"I feel a little better every day, especially now that you're working on things. Have you found out anything?"

"Nothing solid, except that Floretta Bishop's story has some odd holes in it." He gave Pearl a rundown on the "coloreds" under the streetlight. "I'm going to see her again today and try to pin her down. Meanwhile: Did Link ever show you the *Bay Psalm Book*?"

"No. He wasn't much interested in it, and neither was I."

"Well, have you any idea—even a wild speculation—why he had it with him that night?"

"No. I've wondered about that myself. I just chalked it up to his eccentricity. But think of the risk!"

"Okay, one last thing. Link started to write me a strange note the day before he was killed. Let me read it to you, what there is of it."

He read her the fragmentary lines, translating the Latin. "Does that ring any bells, Pearl?"

"Winthrop's laurels? Well, he wheeled and dealed the nomination out of his party, and he's coming up steadily in the polls. As for the rest of it—Dad didn't trust the man, no matter what gifts he brought."

"I've known that for a long time, so why would Link be repeating it to me in a note?"

"I guess we'll never know, since he didn't finish it."

"I suppose not. Well, I better let you go."

"Bless you, Cliff. Take care, and keep me posted."

He hung up and, like Bertie Wooster, proceeded to prong a moody forkful of eggs and b.

If it hadn't been so far and the sunshine so warm, he would have walked to Floretta Bishop's place; but he drove, and he rang her bell at nine o'clock. Yu Shan berf-berfed from his pagoda to the door and stood beside his mistress, prepared to nip ankles, when she opened it.

"Good morning, Mrs. Bishop."

"Hello." She made no move to invite him in.

"Very effective watchdog you have there. He must be a comfort to you in these hazardous times."

"What is it you want, Dr. Dunbar?"

"Oh—well—matter of fact, I'd like to ask you a few more questions if I may. Certain points of your story—your account—of what happened that night seem a little mixed up, even contradictory. I was hoping you could straighten them out. May I come in?"

Her eyes narrowed, and Cliff could hear the breath moving through her nostrils.

"I don't believe that will be necessary."

"I suppose not, if you don't mind talking here. I'm sorry to bother you again."

"Look, Dr. Dunbar, I know you'd like to help run down the men who killed your friend, so I didn't mind playing Dick Tracy and Junior with you once. But enough is enough."

"Mrs. Bishop—that streetlight you stood under was shot out by a little boy two hours before the murder."

She drew a sharp breath and her eyes glittered. "Now, look! I saw the two coloreds. I found the body. I called the cops. That's all I know, and it's all you need to know. If you want to find the killers, go down to Watts. You won't find them by nosing around Westwood."

"Where *were* you standing, Mrs. Bishop?"

She tightened her lips and closed the door. Cliff wasn't sure what emotion inspired her last intense glance at him. His common sense said anger, but his detective urge wanted it to be fear, because fear implied concealment, and concealment implied clues. He decided in favor of fear, because without Floretta he had nothing at all to go on. It might be interesting to find out something about her.

He drove to a Thrifty drugstore in Westwood Village and went to the pay phone, and called Phil Fixico's office.

"Black Artists."

"Phil Fixico, please."

"May I ask who's calling?"

"Tell him it's Jungle Jim."

Brief pause, nice recovery.

"One moment."

Fixico's exuberant voice hit his ear. "Hey, Cliff! How the hell are you?"

"Hi, Phil. How's business?"

"You might say it's in the black. What's happenin'?"

"I'm playing detective, trying to find out who killed Lincoln Schofield. The police seem to have given up."

"Oh, yeah. Your librarian friend. That was a bad scene. But what can I do for you?"

"Pull me out of the river again, I hope. I've only got one lead, a woman named Floretta Bishop, about sixty, who says she used to be an entertainment manager. Her story's fishy and I thought I'd check her out with you, you being in the business."

"That's like asking me if I know Joe Blow in New York."

"I know. It's just a long shot."

"However, hang on a minute. I've got a couple of old directories I can try."

Cliff hung on for several minutes. Ma Bell requested and got another quarter.

"Nothing here, Cliff, but I've got a young actor sitting across from me right now—a *very* promising, *up-and-coming* young actor who's going to make a lot of *money* if he'll just *listen* to me—who says he thinks he's heard the name in Vegas, but that's all he can remember."

"There've been a lot of entertainment managers in Vegas. Where would you suggest I go from here?"

"Maybe she's been in the news. Have you tried the *L.A. Times* morgue?"

"Great idea. I'll give it a try."

"Okay. Stay in touch now."

"We'll get together soon. Many thanks, Phil."

"*Por nada.*"

For what good it would do, which was about zero, there was a smog alert in Los Angeles that day. To postpone or even escape the hell of driving to downtown Los Angeles on the Hollywood Freeway, at the risk of achieving nothing, Cliff returned to the university library and went into the Reference Section to consult the indexes to periodicals.

Some of them seemed to have been moved. A librarian, seeing him in a quandary, asked if he needed help. She was a tiny Chinese-American girl whose nameplate identified her as Shirley Mow.

"Do you know what they've done with the *Los Angeles Times Index?*"

"Oh, yes. Come with me."

He followed her to a cubicle in a corner of the Reference Room, where the long rows of red-bound volumes stood on open shelves next to a computer terminal.

"We thought this was a good way to let people know we have a new on-line periodical search," she said. "The computer saves an awful lot of thumbing through pages—and missing entries."

"You mean you can keyboard somebody's name and it gives you all the newspaper references?"

"Page numbers and all. Are you a faculty member? Yes? Then there'll be no charge. What name do you want to look up?"

"Floretta Bishop."

He spelled "Floretta" for her, and she pressed a button marked "On/Off" and another marked "Local." Lights went on. She dialed a number on her telephone and input a password to the computer. Instructions appeared on the green-lit screen. "Please type your terminal identifier ... Please log in."

Shirley complied and then typed, "A//TERMS A//BISHOP, FLORETTA PER." In a microsecond or two the computer replied, "NOT IN FILE."

"Nothing there," said Cliff.

"Well, this file only goes back to 1977. We have a contract with another information service whose database goes back to 1969. Would that help you?"

"I don't know. Let's give it a try."

She punched more buttons.

"SEARCH MODE," said the words on the screen. "ENTER QUERY."

"1: FLORETTA ADJ BISHOP."

"What's ADJ?" asked Cliff.

"Adjacent. Just a code convention."

The numeral "3" appeared on the screen under Floretta's name.

"Three items," said Shirley. "Would you like a hard copy?"

"Please."

Shirley activated an offline printer resembling a typewriter and requested "ALL/DOC = 3" from the computer.

"ABS NUM 017764293," it responded.

"Abstract number," said Shirley.

And then Cliff's eyes very nearly popped out. Printing several lines per second, the terminal unloaded its gossip.

Title: Las Vegas Madam Held in Shooting Death. Date: 3/17/74. BC Los Angeles Times (LAT) 1974-03-17, Section 1, Page 3, Col. 7. ABS Floretta Bishop, madam of "Rancho Plaisir," arrested in shooting of Mobster Meyer "Socks" Lapidus at her desert brothel. Released on habeas corpus submitted by her attorney, G. Frederick Collins. At arraignment she claims self-defense. Dist. Atty. Roger Lapham contends it was gangland killing, enters first-degree murder charge. Name data: Bishop, Floretta. Lapidus, Meyer "Socks." Lapham, Roger. Collins, G. Frederick. Geo data: Las Vegas.

Computers not being susceptible to surprise nor having to pause for breath, the printer clacked relentlessly on:

ABS NUM 023545991. Title: Murder Trial of Las Vegas Madam Opens. Date: 5/22/74. BC Los Angeles

Times (LAT) 1974-05-22, Section 1, Page 7, Col. 1. ABS murder trial of brothel proprietor Floretta Bishop began today with fiery charges and countercharges on both sides. Prosecution contends Bishop cold-bloodedly eliminated silent partner Meyer "Socks" Lapidus from lucrative business where "attractive starlets" helped patrons to "act out their fantasies." Defense atty. G. Frederick Collins, Ms. Bishop's cousin, denied Lapidus' partnership, presented evidence that Lapidus was trying to muscle in on "Rancho Plaisir" and sell "protection," attacked Bishop with knife when she rebuffed him. Bishop pumped four shots into deceased from .38 Smith & Wesson Police Special. Defendant appeared in court with bruised face, foot-long recent scar on arm. Her story corroborated by two of her "starlets."

The final news item recounted her acquittal by the jury, which had deliberated for thirty-five minutes.

"Is that what you were looking for?" asked Shirley.

Cliff, still awed, gaped at her. "Shirley," he said, "a few years ago two rockhounds looking for specimens in Red Rock Canyon above Mojave stumbled on a gold nugget that weighed twenty-three hundred ounces."

"Twenty-three *hundred*?"

He nodded. "In a dry streambed. Now I know exactly how they felt. I need to sit down, Shirley, and mull."

Leaving the puzzled but pleased librarian behind him, he went out in front of the building, perched on one of the granite blocks flanking the library steps, and lit a Camel—rather furtively, because he had been intending to quit, and two passing rosy-cheeked coeds wearing hiking boots and Bavarian rucksacks shot him disgusted looks.

Some pieces had fallen into place. Floretta appeared to be something more than an innocent bystander. Now, how about the book? Perhaps it was time for a new and closer look. He field-stripped his Camel, dropped the shreds into the bushes, and returned to Special Collections.

"Akira, could I take a look at the *Bay Psalm Book*?"

"Sure thing." Akira took a bunch of keys from his desk and opened the Yale lock of a glass-fronted, metal-barred bookcase. "Here you are. . . . Wait a minute. Do you have any pens on you?"

"A ballpoint."

"I'll have to hold it till you leave. If you want to make any notes you'll have to use a pencil."

Cliff handed over his ballpoint with a smile. "You don't trust anybody, do you?"

"Nope. Not around books. I run a tight ship."

The book had been rebound in full calf at some point in its life—probably in the 1870s, to judge from the style of binding, the age of the leather, and the typeface used to stamp the words "Bay Psalm Book" on the spine in gold letters. A splotch darkened the leather on a corner of the front cover, and the same stain left a rusty brown discoloration on the bottom edge of the book paper. Cliff frowned.

"Yeah, I know," said Akira. "I cleaned it up as best I could. I also had to enter a description of those stains in my records." An angry glint flickered in his eyes. "Any leads yet on who did this?"

"Let's say I have a thread to hang onto between one thumb and forefinger."

Cliff sat down at a reading table near a blond girl in horn-rimmed glasses who seemed to be desperately searching for neologisms in Cavendish's *Life of Wolsey*. He felt like telling her it was no use—Cavendish was possibly the least innovative man in the English Renaissance. Ah, well.

Upon opening the *Bay Psalm Book* to the title page, he noted once again a fact that few people knew. In spite of its popular name and in spite of the words stamped on the spine, the title is not the *Bay Psalm Book* but *The Whole Booke of Psalmes Faithfully Translated into English Metre*. It got its popular name from its having been published in the Massachusetts Bay Colony.

Cliff leafed slowly through the pages, reading occasional

passages in the doggerel verse into which the Psalms had been rendered. The type was uneven because of the metal letters' jostling about in the chase. They couldn't machine to fine tolerances in those days. The paper, however, was the superb pure rag found in old books—sturdy, laid paper, still fresh, with no trace of the yellowing characteristic of modern wood-pulp paper or of the coffee brown afflicting the awful paper the Victorians made when they discovered African esparto grass. You scarcely dare turn the pages of many cheap Victorian books because the paper will shatter like piecrust under your fingers.

Cliff reached the last page, on which the printer had listed errata, typographical errors that had escaped his notice in the printing. Cliff checked two or three of them and saw that they were accurately pointed out.

There was nothing suspicious about the book itself.

Then what *was* suspicious? Nothing.

What about Floretta Bishop?

What about her? She evidently had nothing to do with this. All right, she was a whorehouse madam, but as everyone knows, behind that Smith & Wesson Police Special beats a heart of gold.

Exasperated at returning to square one, Cliff shook out a second Camel from his pack.

"Ah—ah!" said a voice over his shoulder.

"Sorry, Akira. Forgot."

"What did you find out?"

"Not a damn thing."

"No scraps of paper bearing secret codes?"

"Nope, and no matchbook covers, motel keys, torn dollar bills, or exotic cigarette ashes."

"Thanks to me. Where do you go from here?"

"Hughes Market."

"How come?"

"I need groceries."

THE

VVHOLE

BOOKE OF PSALMES

Faithfully
TRANSLATED *into* ENGLISH
Metre.

Whereunto is prefixed a difcourfe de-
claring not only the lawfullnes, but alfo
the neceffity of the heavenly Ordinance
of finging Scripture Pfalmes in
the Churches of
God.

Coll. III.

Let the word of God dwell plenteoufly in
you, in all wifdome, teaching and exhort-
ing one another in Pfalmes, Himnes, and
fpirituall Songs, finging to the Lord with
grace in your hearts.

Iames v.
If any be afflicted, let him pray, and if
any be merry let him fing pfalmes.

Imprinted
1640

FIVE

*A*mong the fresh vegetables Cliff put in the lower bin of his refrigerator was a bunch of parsley almost as green as the snow-cone juice on the fat boy's face. Although most Americans think of parsley as a mere touch of color that restaurants brighten their entrées with, Cliff always ate his. He liked its texture and its zingy mint tang, but he also knew that parsley is loaded with iron and vitamins. Nevertheless, he felt self-conscious when he ate it in public, resenting the startled looks people always gave him, as if a browsing goat had wandered in among them.

He reflected on that experience with irritation as he went out to his car for the bags of canned goods. Dumb clucks. The Greeks knew better. They prized parsley highly—*ta kalà selina*, they called it. "Where are my roses? Where is my beautiful parsley?" went a children's rhyme in ancient Athens. Indeed, at the Corinthian games, athletes were crowned with a wreath of parsley instead of a wreath of laurel, or bay.

Bay? For Pete's sake, are we back on that again? He rubbed his jaw in irritation. *All right, then, let's give this some concentrated thought.* What was Link trying to say?

For starters, he went into his library and looked up "Bay-tree: flourishing like a green b." in the *Oxford Dictionary of Quotations*. He was surprised to find that it came from Psalm 34: "I myself have seen the ungodly in great power: and flourishing like a green bay-tree."

Okay, so Link didn't like Winthrop. What else is new? "I fear Greeks bearing gifts." Link certainly wasn't afraid of Winthrop; however, he was equating the *Bay Psalm Book* with the Trojan horse. In a way, that was valid: Winthrop was using his donation as a ploy to help him win the election.

He took Link's note out again and reread it. "As of today, however, *timeo Danaos et dona ferentis.*" Why *as of today*? The only explanation Cliff could think of was that, on the day Link typed the note, he had come to regard the book as a Trojan horse—maybe a wooden horse? An imitation horse? If that interpretation were correct, there may have been something to Cliff's original, facetious shot in the dark: In spite of the evidence, perhaps Link suspected the book was a fake. At least that could explain why he treated it so cavalierly that day, toting it around with him, even taking it home. If the book was a fake, it would have to be a pretty old one, perhaps from 1870, assuming the same age as the binding.

He inserted a sheet of paper into his typewriter and wrote to C. T. Post at Harvard, tactfully asking what tests of authenticity Post had performed on the book, and what features, if any, disturbed him or at least made him do some double checking.

He felt rather foolish doing it, but nothing ventured, nothing gained.

In the morning he telephoned Bradford Silliman at Stanford's English Department. To Cliff's surprise, an impatient voice answered, "Silliman here."

"Hello, Dr. Silliman. This is Clifford Dunbar of LAU's English Department."

"I know of you. What do you want?"

"I'd like to ask you a few questions about your appraisal of the *Bay Psalm Book.*"

Whatever for? See here, Dr. Dunbar, I'm very busy. I'm due to give a final exam in bibliography in fifteen minutes. I intend to read the blue books by the end of the day. Tonight I'm packing, tomorrow morning I will turn in my course grades, and tomorrow afternoon I am flying to England to spend my sabbatical year at the Bodleian. Now, what sort of thing did you want to ask about the *Bay Psalm Book*?"

"I have some doubts about its authenticity."

"Oh, for pity's sake! Nonsense! Post and I examined it thoroughly."

"I know that, but I'd like to go over your evidence with you anyway."

"I'm sorry, but I simply have no time."

"Could you call me collect here when you have a moment?"

"I prefer not to commit myself to that."

"Could I come see you, then?"

A pause ensued, followed by a loud exhalation of breath.

"I'll be in my office at some point between nine and ten tomorrow morning. If you care to wait I can spare you half an hour, but I assure you you're on a wild-goose chase. However, it's your money."

"Thank you very much. I'll be there."

He was lucky enough to get a bad seat in the tail section of an Air California plane to San Jose that evening. He rented a car there and drove the freeway to Redwood City, where he didn't see any redwoods, took an offramp, and followed El Camino Real until he found a motel with a vacancy sign, checked in, and went out to dinner.

He wasn't really hungry, but he stumbled onto a small neighborhood restaurant of the sort, rare these days, that featured a typewritten menu, fresh vegetables, and home cooking. With a smile, he passed over the "soup *de jour* of the day" and chose the "sirlion steak" with peas and carrots. They were surprisingly good.

The Seven Seas Motel, however, made him glad he wasn't a professional detective, traveling salesman, or other itinerant who had to roost in such places. Of the Seven, though with geographic inexactness, Cliff's room apparently belonged to the China Sea. A red-orange table lamp with fake Chinese characters on its ceramic base was screwed to the bedside table. An abused TV set stood in a corner locked to its mount. The headboard of the bed, upholstered in green, rose nearly to the ceiling, where it broke out into a tiny canopy projecting six inches from the wall and adorned with upward-curving corners from which dangled red nylon balls, dusty. On the opposite wall, above the bureau, hung two fake Chinese watercolors in trapezoidal frames (the mysterious East), depicting two reassuringly Caucasian girls in flowing Oriental gowns. One looked like Lily Pons, the other like Elizabeth Taylor. Probably underestimating the taste of the American public, the proprietor had screwed the pictures to the wall, too.

Floretta's peke would have felt right at home. Cliff felt much less so. He read Wodehouse for a while and finally dropped off to sleep, alternately resenting Silliman and longing for Carole.

Cliff was glad to get away in the morning. He drove to the Stanford campus and asked his way to the English Department. The campus was gorgeous with flowers and trees in full summer bloom and leaf. As usual, he was surprised to rediscover how tall the trees were, here to the north.

Another surprise awaited him when he entered Bradford Silliman's office. The man who rose to greet him was not at all the skinny, mincing fop with a keyhole of a mouth that he had pictured during their phone conversation. On the contrary, Silliman was a huge man with a body like a wine vat, hair receding from a bulging intellectual forehead, and a jaw that could crack hickory nuts. The eyes that he fixed on Cliff snapped, making constant little darts—up, down, right, left— of perhaps a sixteenth of an inch. Cliff guessed that Silliman was a man who thought fast and accurately, was impatient with slower-moving or negligent minds, and no doubt was a tough taskmaster for students of bibliography—which was all to the good, because bibliography, if it is to be at all respectable, demands thoroughness and meticulous attention to detail.

The introductory amenities were over in a trice. Silliman had little tolerance for ritual niceties.

"And now, Dr. Dunbar, what is this nonsense about the *Bay Psalm Book?*"

"It appears that Lincoln Schofield suspected it's a forgery."

"Well, if he did he was a fool! I told you on the phone that both Post and I gave it a thorough examination. There's no question of its authenticity."

"I know, but a second look wouldn't do any harm."

"By whom? I'm certainly not going to. Why don't you examine it yourself? You're a bibliographer, aren't you?"

"It's not my specialty. I teach it, but my emphasis is on bibliography as a tool for scholarly research. I'm not all that strong on the physical characteristics of books."

"You mean you taught it, don't you? I've heard that you're leaving your department."

"That's true."

"Hmph. Well."

"The day before he was murdered, Link began a note to me that he never finished. It was cryptic, but it strongly implied that he thought the book was a reproduction—a superb fake, but a fake nonetheless."

"On what evidence?"

"I don't know."

"Oh, now, really Dr. Dunbar! Look—to stop wasting time for both of us, let me . . . see here, are you familiar with Carter and Pollard's *An Inquiry into the Nature of Certain Nineteenth-Century Pamphlets?*"

"Of course—dealing with the Thomas Wise forgeries."

"Correct. I applied their tests to the *Bay Psalm Book*, all the ones that were relevant. Pardon me if I insult your intelligence, but it will save time if I assume you're ignorant."

"You're not far off. Shoot."

Silliman gave him a squirrelly look and went on.

"First, provenance: Not solid proof, of course, but Winthrops have been in Massachusetts since early colonial times, and Perry Winthrop says that the copy has always been in the family library. That is eminently logical."

Cliff nodded.

"Second, the paper: There is no doubt whatever that the paper is genuine seventeenth-century rag brought from England. To make sure, I examined it under a microscope, and there was not a trace of wood pulp or esparto grass. If there had been chemical wood, the paper could have been made no earlier than 1874; and esparto grass was used commercially only beginning in 1861. So the paper is genuine."

"Couldn't a forger find the right paper somewhere?"

"It's been done, on a small scale—as that man did who turned out all those Abraham Lincoln forgeries on the correct blue paper that he found. But those were only a few single sheets. One certainly can't drop into the nearest stationer's and pick up a ream or so, can one?"

"Hardly."

"Third, the typography. Naturally, I gave it severe scrutiny, and the font is genuine. For one thing, I looked for kernless f's and j's. Do you know what I'm talking about?"

"Yes, putting crooks in their backs so no part of the letter sticks out over the body of the typeface. The loops on the kerned f's and j's were always breaking off in the press."

"Precisely. Kernless letters date no later than 1880. None of them appear in the *Bay Psalm Book*. All the f's and j's are kerned. Last, both Post and I did a side-by-side comparison of the Winthrop copy with an unquestionably authentic 1640 edition at Yale. They were as identical as they could be, considering the looseness of those old presses."

"Did you run across anything at all suspicious?"

"Nothing whatever."

"I suppose Perry Winthrop paid you a healthy fee for your opinion?"

Silliman froze, his nostrils flaring.

"If that question, Dr. Dunbar, implies what I assume it implies, you will please leave my office."

"No offense at all. Merely asking. I just don't know what the practice is."

"Of course I was paid! I'm not such a fool as to do appraisals for nothing. If it's any business of yours, Mr. Winthrop was quite generous, and I look forward to seeing him as governor in Sacramento."

"That looks probable, for better or for worse."

"Anything is better than the wild man we have now. And now, if you'll excuse me, I have a very busy day ahead of me."

"I was hoping to dig a little deeper into a few questions."

"I'm sure you were, but any further excavation is up to you."

Silliman rose and began stuffing books and papers into his briefcase.

The man's tone was so insulting that Cliff had to fight an urge to slug him one. It stuck in his craw to toady to the pompous bastard, but obviously it was time to win friends and influence people.

Rising himself, Cliff said, "By the way, Dr. Silliman, a couple of summers ago I backpacked from Sequoia to Kings Canyon and stopped off on the way to climb Mount Silliman. I'd be interested to know if it was named after someone in your family."

"It was indeed. It was named after Benjamin Silliman, a great-great uncle of mine. He was a professor of chemistry at Yale around the time of the Civil War. So you've been up there? I've never seen it myself."

"You really should go. You'd feel honored. It's a beautiful peak, jutting up from Silliman Crest, which is pure, gleaming white granite."

"There's a Silliman Crest, too?"

"And a Silliman Lake, a Silliman Meadow, a Silliman Creek, and a Silliman Pass. Your family has something of a monopoly on the area."

"Well, well, well! I must try that sometime—go up with a camera—although I fear I'm not much of one for the outdoors, leading the *vita contemplativa* as I do."

"You might even climb Mount Silliman. It's not too difficult from the south face. The north face is nearly straight up and down."

"No, thank you! I'll content myself with a photograph."

"Probably a wise decision. Well, thank you for your time. It's been a pleasure to touch bases with a genuine Silliman."

"Those other questions that were bothering you, Dr. Dunbar. Can you tell me briefly what they are?"

"Oh, that. It's only one broad question, really. I was going to ask you: If you were forced to play devil's advocate and launch a purely cynical, one-sided attack on the Winthrop copy, what would you pick on?"

"Ah. Hm. Well. Although the book *is* genuine, mind you, two or three little points bothered me when I first examined it, but they came to nothing."

"Such as?"

"Oh, the nineteenth-century binding, for example. Ordinarily, books have to be rebound only when they've been used a great deal or they've been badly treated. That was not the case here. The rest of the book was in superb condition. No pen or pencil marks, no underlining, no pages missing, perhaps a corner torn off here and there, but one wonders why it was necessary to rebind at all. Of course, the old binding may simply have dried up and fallen apart, or someone may have dropped it on the floor and damaged it beyond repair. Why are you smiling?"

"I just thought of the old saying that you can't judge a book by its cover."

"Precisely why I dismissed it. Besides, other copies of the book have been rebound. I was also surprised to find no foxing at all. Again, pardon me if I'm teaching my grandmother to suck eggs, but foxing occurs when tiny particles of iron from the printing press are embedded in the paper and then rust, speckling both that page and usually the facing page with brown flecks. Steel engravings are most notorious for that, but of course the *Bay Psalm Book* has no engravings. Nothing but some border decorations on the title page. However, that proves nothing at all. I have seen books printed in Venice by Aldus Manutius dating from 1500 that didn't have a speck of foxing. So where does that leave us?"

"Wary, but still convinced?"

"Exactly."

"How closely did you examine the text?"

"I read through a great deal of it and checked the errata list at the end. Nothing more was necessary, in my opinion. Besides, the Psalms are rendered into frightful doggerel."

"You didn't actually proofread the book, then?"

"Heavens, no!"

"Did Mr. Winthrop have any letters or documents that back up the provenance of the book?"

"No. It would have been convenient if he had, but then the book has always been in the family, and one doesn't ordinarily chitchat about one's books in letters unless, perhaps, one is a book collector—or bibliographer. And now I really must go. I hope I've been of some help to you."

"You have indeed."

"And let me know if you plan to go up to Mount Silliman again. Who knows? I just might be tempted to melt some of this too, too solid flesh and, ah, try to rise to new heights, so to speak. *Per ardua ad astra.*"

"Let's do that. And you'll find that the *ardua* aren't too rough. It's only about five or six miles from Lodgepole Campground in Sequoia up to Silliman Pass."

"Excellent. Next year, perhaps."

"August or early September. We'll give it a try."

"Let me know how your search comes out. I can't find it in me to wish you luck, and I'm afraid you're chasing a wild goose, but you can write me care of the Bodleian."

SIX

*I*t took Cliff thirty-five minutes to fly from San Jose to Los Angeles International, but eighty minutes for him to collect his suitcase and drive the San Diego Freeway to the LAU campus. He walked into the offices of the university press at ten minutes before twelve and found Jim Bobrow in a rage, riffling through the final pages of a manuscript before he went to lunch.

"Hello, Cliff," Bobrow growled.

"Hi, Jim. What's the trouble?"

"Someday—*someday*—one of these professors is going to have a mental lapse and accidentally write a book in plain English, and this press will at long last have a best seller on its hands. Here's a guy with some good ideas on how to start eliminating racial segregation in Los Angeles—and listen to how the bozo writes: 'In addition to the restrictive impact of segregation on the exercise of nonwhite households' residential location selection calculus, there exists a corresponding effect on the white calculus.' "

"White calculus? Isn't that the stuff that collects on your teeth?"

Bobrow glowered and read on. " 'Many whites associate a disutility to residential proximity to nonwhites.' "

"Don't spoil my lunch."

"Why not? It's ruined mine. Not only that, this guy doesn't like to be edited, because he claims editors 'distort his meaning.' Jesus. And what do *you* want?"

"A proofreader. Who's the best proofreader you've got?"

"Mona Moore, hands down. And you keep your hands off her. You aren't going to steal her from me."

"Don't worry. I just want to borrow her for a free-lance job if I can."

"Sure. She could use the money."

"Where'll I find her?"

"Down the hall, third door to the left."

The door was open. A young woman of twenty-six or so sat at a desk with a red pencil in her hand, peering alternately at a sheet of blue-and-white-striped computer printout paper and a marked-up typewritten manuscript.

Cliff knocked lightly on the doorjamb. The young woman looked up at him through glasses with light blue plastic frames. A disorderly mass of tight, sunburned, blond curls surrounded her face. She wore no makeup and she had a house painter's white coveralls over her dress. Around her neck was a necklace of eucalyptus seedpods.

"Miss Moore?"

"Yes."

"Am I interrupting you?"

"Of course."

"Oh, I'm sorry."

"That's all right. I want to be interrupted. It's lunchtime."

"I'm Clifford Dunbar."

"From the English Department?"

"For the next two or three weeks, yes."

"What did you want to see me about?"

"Jim Bobrow referred me to you. I need a crack proofreader for a very special job."

"How much will it pay?"

"If you're as good as Jim says you are, twenty-five dollars an hour."

"I am, I am! For twenty-five an hour I'd be willing to proof letter by letter!"

"Believe it or not, that's just about what I have in mind— which is why the pay is so high. I don't ordinarily throw money around like a drunken sailor."

"You're certainly no tightwad, either. You're a loosewad, if there is such a word."

"There isn't. Shall I tell you about the job?"

"No. Not yet. I want to roll that twenty-five dollars an hour around in my head for a minute or two."

He smiled. A small sign thumbtacked to the wall above her desk caught his eye: "Mona Moore—proofreading at it's best." He chuckled.

"Aha! You got it!" she said. "But of course an English teacher would. I use that as a quick spot-check. When someone doesn't get it, I know I'm dealing with a person who's either illiterate or unobservant."

"Glad I passed. Look here, could I take you to lunch? We could talk about the proofreading job."

"I get a free lunch, too? You're on, Dr. Dunbar."

"Cliff. I use 'Doctor' only when I need to intimidate students or make reservations in Las Vegas."

"All right, Cliff. We're off." She stepped out of the coveralls and took up her purse.

The host at the Hamburger Hamlet in Westwood Village escorted them to a corner booth and gave them menus.

"Don't stint," said Cliff.

"I don't intend to. This is my chance to break out of the graduate student's spaghetti-wienie-enchilada modality."

She ordered a top sirloin steak, medium rare, he a chef's salad. Mona took her glasses off. He noted that her eyes were a cool green, that her face was heart-shaped and sprinkled with freckles across her upper cheeks and nose, and that if you looked at her two or three times you realized she was rather pretty—a daisy, perhaps, compared with a hothouse rose— but also that without the twinkling intelligence in her eyes, she could have been taken for plain.

He was glad she had shed the coveralls, but the eucalyptus pods on a furry brown string still bothered him a trifle. Only recently had students started breaking away from the godaw- ful clothes and grime that were a legacy from hippie days. He remembered a coed from Beverly Hills in one of his classes who wore a pendant made from a rusty can lid with a hole punched in it, strung on a rawhide thong. She had found the piece of tin in a parking lot, where cars had been running over it, and pounced on it as a piece of *art trouvé*.

Mona put her glasses into her purse and looked up at him, her green eyes shaded by long brown eyelashes. Seeing him appraising her, she said pleasantly, "I should warn you that if you tell me how much prettier I am without my glasses, I plan to kick you in the shins, and I'm wearing stout shoes."

"Okay, I won't."

"You won't?"

"Not if you say so."

"Aw, go ahead!"

"Well, you are."

"Thanks."

"What I was really thinking, though, was that you're the first girl named Mona that I've actually met."

"Oh, that! My name came out of my parents' perverted sense of humor. My mother majored in French in college and she taught my father, and they're both crazy about anything French. They have a favorite song that Jean Sablon used to sing, and in it is the line, 'Viens plus près, mon amour, ton coeur contre mon coeur.' So they had the brilliant idea of naming me Mona Moore."

"I think that's clever—and charming."

"Well, I think it's dumb. I hope to get even with them by marrying a man named Wojtulewicz."

"Where are you from originally?"

"Madras, Oregon. It's on the eastern side of the Cascades, close to the Deschutes River. My father teaches high school English there. And history, in a pinch."

"I suppose you're an English major yourself."

"No—physical therapy."

"Where did the proofreading come from, then?"

"I don't know. I just have a keen eye for detail, somehow. Maybe I got it from Dad. He taught me to read early, and I've always been word-conscious. I proofread everything I see. Did you notice they spelled it 'irresistable" on the menu?"

"No, but I recently had a 'sirlion steak' near Redwood City."

She laughed delightedly. "Oh, you can get that in every small town in Oregon! And how about this proofreading job? Is it a book of yours, or a scholarly article for a journal?"

"Far from it. Do you know about the *Bay Psalm Book* the library acquired not long ago?"

She did, and she remembered that Lincoln Schofield had it with him the night he was murdered.

"I have strong reason to believe Link thought the book was a fake—a brilliant forgery. Don't ask me why."

"Do you think it had anything to do with his murder?"

"Probably not. They're probably two separate events, and I'm investigating both of them. The only lead I have on the murder is a very colorful woman named Floretta Bishop, an ex-brothel-madam from Las Vegas."

She listened with fascination to his rundown on Floretta and commented, "Maybe she killed him herself."

"Possible but not likely, although she did shoot that hood to death in Las Vegas. But how would she get rid of the knife right there on the scene?"

"Throw it in the ivy."

"Hey, not bad! I wonder if the police searched there."

"You mean there actually was ivy?"

"A whole bed of it out on the boulevard strip. However, if you're going to kill somebody, you don't take your doggie along. So let's get back to the proofreading. What I plan to do is have you sit in Special Collections with the Winthrop *Bay Psalm Book* and a facsimile reprint of a genuine copy and compare them carefully—phrase for phrase, word for word, even letter by letter if necessary."

"Why letter by letter?"

"First of all, because half of the words in the darned book have very peculiar spellings. Anything that came out of the author's pen was okay with him. He spells 'solid' with two l's, 'far' with two r's and an e, 'we' with two e's, and so on—and he isn't consistent. So you can't just look for misspelled words—most of 'em *are* misspelled. You have to see if the misspelled words match."

"That's going to slow me down to a snail's pace."

"Afraid so. And then there's the type font."

Cliff repeated the lesson about the kerned and kernless f's and j's. "But concentrate on the text and save that sort of thing for the end. We can always look at the type font as a separate job."

"Where do we get the facsimile reprint?"

"The library's had one for years. It was printed by Dodd, Mead in New York in 1903. It's actually a composite of one copy of the *Bay Psalm Book* in private hands and one in the Lenox Branch of the New York Public Library—at least it was in 1903."

"This sounds like real fun."

"It also sounds like real eyestrain; and we don't want you to ruin those green eyes that you're so much prettier with without your glasses, do we?"

"Spoken like a true grammarian."

"Anyway, look for discrepancies of any kind: typographical errors that appear in one version and not the other, omissions, lower-case letters that should be caps, American spellings that should be British—'colour,' 'honour,' 'analyse,' such things as that."

"If the book is a forgery, shouldn't it be pretty easy to detect?"

"You may find the book *isn't* a forgery. The two foremost bibliographers in the country have certified it as genuine—but then they didn't proofread it. At least Silliman up at Stanford didn't."

"But if it *is* a forgery, seems to me it ought to be easy to prove. I know from my own experience that no matter how painstaking you are in proofreading, you can just about count on missing at least one typo every fifty pages."

"True—but there have been perfect books, like the Bible."

"But has there ever been a perfect forgery?"

"I only know of one, and it wasn't a book. I read about a French stamp collector who was cheated by a stamp company when he was a little boy. It made him so mad he developed a mania on the subject. For years and years he studied chemistry, engraving, papermaking, printing, inks, gum-making, God knows what-all—and then he started forging rare stamps, which he sold a few at a time to stamp dealers in Paris at terrific prices. When he finally amassed a fortune, he stuck the knife in and twisted it: He announced that the stamps were forgeries."

"What did they do to him?"

"Not a damn thing. They couldn't. All those dealers and their customers were frantic. They ran their stamps through every test known to man, and they couldn't identify this guy's forgeries. They were so perfect that even the forger himself couldn't tell them apart!"

"Yes, but a whole book is a different matter, isn't it? To carry off a *tour de force* like that—what kind of motivation would it take? It seems to me the forger would have to be both a raving maniac and a fantastic perfectionist."

"And one hell of a craftsman."

"There's one other thing I'll bet you haven't thought of," said Mona. "What if it turns out the book *was* forged—but it was forged fifty years ago? What does that do to your case?"

Cliff frowned. "I don't know. I hadn't thought of that."

"That isn't exactly catching the forger."

"I know it isn't. I'd be right back with Floretta Bishop and her Mutt and Jeff story. Damn it, Mona, I'm beginning to think you're too intelligent."

He rubbed his scar in irritation.

"How did you get that?" Mona asked.

"Fell off my tricycle when I was three."

"No, seriously."

"Vietnam."

"Oh."

"Are you shocked? Disappointed?"

"No. Vietnam was anything but a clear-cut issue."

"I agree. I was a real hawk at first—you know the line: Why shouldn't the Communists break down instead of us? But then I saw all the pimples on the pickle we had gotten ourselves into and I did a flipflop. Instead of trying to win a war, I focused on getting my men and myself out of there with a whole skin."

"Did you?"

"I lost a few."

"And you picked up a scar. It gives you character."

"Think so?"

"Did you see *On the Waterfront*?"

"Sure."

"Remember that scene where Brando is talking with Eva Marie Saint with half his face in light and half in shadow? Good and evil? That's sort of what it does to you. The left side of your face looks like an Eagle Scout, and the right side is really sinister."

"I'm well aware of that. And I'm just devious enough to switch 'em back and forth when it's to my advantage. I'm that way inside too, you know."

"Aren't we all?"

"Just so you know."

"I know I'd hate to have you really mad at me."

"Don't worry. I don't beat up on women—reactionary as that may sound."

"That's okay with me. We feminists have to draw the line somewhere. Mind if I have dessert?"

"I'd turn sinister if you didn't."

"In that case I'll have a tin-roof sundae."

"What the hell is that?"

"Ice cream, fudge sauce, and a hailstorm of Spanish peanuts."

"I'll join you."

SEVEN

*T*hey walked down the hall together to Special Collections. "You're sure, now, I'm not tearing you away from important work? I don't want Jim Bobrow mad at me."

"It's okay. The professor who wrote the book I'm proofing has gone to Australia to spend the summer on the Great Barrier Reef. He's a marine biologist. We can't print the book anyway until he's checked the galleys."

He introduced her to Akira Yonenaka and was pleased to see that they liked each other right away. Mona cheerfully surrendered her ballpoint pens. Akira gave her the *Bay Psalm Book* and the Dodd, Mead facsimile and began his standard lecture on the rules and regulations of the Special Collections reading room, starting with the no-smoking prohibition.

"I've heard this before," said Cliff. "Mona, you go ahead and familiarize yourself with the book and get a general feeling for the job. Take your time. If you can't start actual proofreading this afternoon, that's all right. I have other things to do. And don't let Akira frighten you."

"Too late. He already has."

"Good!" said Akira. "That means I'm doing my job. Let's get you set up with a reading rack."

Cliff left them and went once more to the Reference Room, where he sought out Shirley Mow.

"Could I get you to work your magic again?"

"Of course, Dr. Dunbar. What would you like to look up?"

"*Bay Psalm Book*—but just for the last year."

She turned her machine on, logged in, and typed, "1___: BAY PSALM BOOK."

"RESULT 14," responded the computer.

"Fourteen items," said Shirley. "Do you want all of them?"

"Please."

"ALL/DOC = 14," she typed, and the printout terminal began spewing whole paragraphs of capital letters onto the roll of white paper, which crawled rapidly upward, toppled, and folded itself neatly in a metal tray. Cliff watched the first item as it went by.

> ABS NUM 099565427. Title: Perry Winthrop to Donate Priceless Book to LAU Library. Date: 10/25/79. BC Los Angeles Times (LAT) 1979-10-25, Section 1, Page 1, Col. 5. ABS Perry Winthrop, who recently announced that he is "thinking about" running for governor of California next year, will donate copy of Bay Psalm Book, first book printed in American colonies, to LAU Library. First edition now valued between $250 thousand and $300 thousand. Winthrop discovered it among books he shipped here from family home in Worcester, Mass., was not aware he had it. "It must have sat there forgotten in the library all these years," he said. An aide noticed it and informed Winthrop of its value, whereupon he decided to donate the book, "if genuine," to LAU, where scholars will have access to it. "Besides," he quipped, "I would be an uneasy guardian, indeed, having a priceless national treasure sitting on my bookshelf where burglars and thieves would have access to it."

"It isn't priceless, you ass," muttered Cliff. "Three hundred thousand is a price."

"I beg your pardon?"

"Just talking to myself, Shirley."

The abstract continued with the information that Winthrop would submit the book to experts for authentication.

Having gotten all the citations, Cliff decided to read them

in full. The next item revealed that the book would be vetted by Silliman and Post at the suggestion of Sidney Marienthal, the LAU university librarian, although Marienthal was also an authority on British and American incunabula and opined that there was no question of the book's authenticity. . . . Whereupon, in the next item, Winthrop's memory of the book clarified considerably. He remembered seeing it in the family library "some years ago" but never paid any attention to it, "my tastes in literature at the time running more to Tom Swift and Percy Keese Fitzhugh." A puzzled but sharp reporter reminded Winthrop that only a week or two previously he had said he didn't know he had the book. "I meant out here in California," Winthrop responded.

Late in November, Silliman and Post announced that the book was genuine, and Winthrop announced that he was tossing his hat in the ring for the gubernatorial nomination— "figuratively speaking, of course, because I discovered to my surprise that men in California don't wear hats." Asked if he didn't agree he was peaking rather early for a candidate, he conceded that he was but explained that he had a great deal to say about the wretched condition the present governor and legislature had gotten California into, and he presented the elaborate plans he had for rescuing the state.

These plans, he said, could be subsumed under the general maxim of "Simplify, simplify, simplify." Government had turned into a monstrous machine that consumed far more than it produced. If you are intent on merely slicing bread, you don't need a giant mechanism with five thousand cams, levers, and servomotors to do it. A bread knife in a man's or a woman's hand will do. He believed that virtually the whole rickety structure of government should be torn down and rebuilt. Departments could be consolidated and eliminated. Most taxes could be done away with if the state instituted a truly progressive, indexed income tax for both individuals and corporations. He would levy much higher "sin taxes"— excise taxes on tobacco, alcohol, and the like. He would

greatly expand the number of personal-damage suits as-
signed to compulsory arbitration, with lawyers and retired
judges acting as arbiters, to unplug the unconscionable bot-
tlenecks in judicial work loads. He believed in strong labor
unions and equally strong management. He contended that
business should not have to pay through the nose for the solid
gold shackles that government clamped to their arms and
legs. On the contrary, if business were more profitable it
could sell at lower prices, people could afford to buy more,
more people would be employed, and even at very low tax
rates state revenues would rise and the state could efficiently
supply needed public services. Crime rates would also drop,
along with the tremendous social costs that crime inflicts. In
short, California needed a new broom.

Asked specifically what departments and programs he
would eliminate, Winthrop said he'd talk about that later in
the campaign after he and his staff, headed by Fred Collins,
his legal and financial adviser, completed their analyses.

Asked if he planned to declare his donation of the *Bay Psalm
Book* as a tax deduction, he replied, "You better believe it. I
don't think anybody should pay taxes he doesn't have to.
Mind you, I'd be happy to make this a purely altruistic gift to
the world of scholarship, but I don't believe I should have to
pay for the privilege of giving something away."

"Right on," said Cliff, reading.

The next cluster of news items revealed the deft hand of
Winthrop's press relations expert at work. In two items, the
man moistened his lips and trumpeted a fanfare to announce
the imminent presentation of the book to the library along
with another classic product of New England thought, a first
edition of Henry Adams's *Mont-St.-Michel and Chartres*. The
orchestrated presentation ceremony followed, illustrated
with three photographs, one of a beaming Winthrop handing
the book to the equally refulgent chancellor of the university,
one of the book's 1640 title page, and one of the invited guests
at the reception, including Link Schofield, with his thumb in

his vest pocket, looking dour, and, in the murky background, Akira Yonenaka and Cliff himself.

Roger Barnsdale, assistant professor of American Literature at LAU, contributed an accompanying article that covered the early history of American printing, the significance of the *Bay Psalm Book* for the study of Puritan culture, an account of the book's decline in popularity, and the fate of the eleven surviving copies of the original printing of one thousand, seven hundred. Until the discovery of the Winthrop copy, only two perfect copies of the book were known to exist, one of them in the Bodleian Library at Oxford. ("I wonder if Silliman will visit it.") "It is miraculous that the Bodleian copy exists at all," wrote Barnsdale, "let alone being perfect, because it belonged to a Bishop Tanner, all of whose books and manuscripts were accidentally dumped into a river while being transported from Norwich to Oxford in 1731. The books remained submerged in the water for twenty hours. . . . In view of the rarity of the book and its historical importance, it is an astounding stroke of good fortune that a perfect copy should have shown up in the Winthrop family library, that Perry Winthrop removed from Massachusetts to California, and that he so generously bestowed the book on Los Angeles University."

It was an impressive article, lively though scholarly, and, reflected Cliff, should help nail down an associate professorship—with the prize of tenure—for Roger. The only point on which Cliff has some disagreement with Roger Barnsdale was his describing Winthrop's move to California as an astounding stroke of good fortune. As opposition newspapers were fond of pointing out, Winthrop left the East Coast because he had a speech impediment called Massachusetts. Every time he made a speech, the metropolitan newspapers panned it— as they did on the occasion when Winthrop casually mentioned that he didn't think child labor was *entirely* bad. After all, children earn money delivering newspapers, mowing lawns, baby-sitting, and selling lemonade. A few hours in a factory would be no worse and would afford the kids the opportunity to learn more useful skills. But no sooner did he say "factory" than he was jumped on from coast to coast, with the newspapers caricaturing him as Squeers of Dotheboys Hall. He never mentioned the subject again.

As an apple tree may sprout in the desert and quickly wither, so it was with Winthrop's career. His venerated name got him elected to a minor state office, and he rose to become attorney general for the Commonwealth of Massachusetts. He could rise no farther. He ran for Congress and lost; he limped for the Senate against a much too popular incumbent. Meanwhile, running for other offices forced him to abandon the attorney generalship, where his record was fair if mixed. His greatest achievement was the establishment of a statewide system of neighborhood judicial boards for settling minor disputes, which won him widespread gratitude from the courts and the citizenry. He gained a reputation as a crime-buster when his office cracked down on reputed Mafia hoodlums during a crime wave that was touched off by a war for the succession to the post of New England *capo*. Suspicion was aroused, however, when nearly all of the hoodlums he convicted proved to belong to only one side in the war: the side that was not expected to win, but did. The new *capo* pulled certain strings; the majority party pulled others; and Winthrop suddenly found himself stranded on the beach at Cape Cod looking for pretty shells.

The astounding stroke of good fortune therefore accrued strictly to Winthrop when he moved to California and found that both the meteorological and political climates agreed with him. The state's politicos of both parties regarded his arrival dubiously, and there were grumblings that Winthrop was merely a carpetbagger, a crass opportunist. When a *Los Angeles Times* reporter asked him pointedly why he abandoned a state where his family had roots three hundred years old, he flashed a mischievous smile and said, "Oh, we Winthrops are just nomads, I suppose." (Laughter.) "First England, then Massachusetts, then California. We just don't seem able to settle down in one place for more than three centuries." The state loved it. Cliff thought it was pretty good himself.

Reading on, he found that Winthrop shed more light— perhaps final, definitive light—on the provenance of the *Bay Psalm Book*.

"It's been in the family as long as I can remember," he said, "but I must confess I never paid much attention to it. It's so hard to read that I contented myself with the King James and Douai versions of the Psalms."

Had this not been California where, as Winthrop had observed, men don't wear hats, and had it not been the Reference Room of the LAU Library, where he wouldn't have been wearing a hat anyway, Cliff would have taken off his hat in admiration of those last remarks. In fifty words or less, Winthrop had nailed down the provenance of the *Bay Psalm Book*; reaffirmed the easy generosity of a wealthy man; established himself as a Bible reader; courted the favor of both Protestants and Catholics; and quashed any speculation that he might be an egghead intellectual. No doubt about it: The man was an impressive politician.

But for the purposes of Cliff's investigation, the most impressive phenomenon was the thematic bridge Winthrop had constructed, running from unawareness of owning the book at one end, to having always been aware of it at the other.

It was time to check back with Mona Moore.

She sat near a window with two reading racks on the table before her. She did not notice Cliff coming in, for her blood was up and she was on the hunt. Her eyes darted from one book to the other, and intelligence played about her face like St. Elmo's fire.

"How's it going?"

"Oh! Hello! Well—I've really just gotten into it. I spent quite a while reading into both copies, sort of acclimating myself."

"Good. Take your time."

"But I've already found something odd."

"No kidding. What is it?"

"Let's see—what's the easiest way to put it? There's a place in the Winthrop copy where there actually *should* have been a typographical error, only there isn't one."

"I don't quite follow that."

Mona turned to the back of the book.

"See here? Stephen Daye, the printer, put an errata sheet at the end listing the typos that he found himself."

Faults escaped in printing.

Escaped.	Right
pſalme 9. vers 9. opreſſ.	oppreſt.
v. 10. knowes.	know.
pſ. 18. w. 29. the.	thee.
w. 31. 3 parts wanting.	3 part.
pſ. 19. w. 13. let thou- kept back.	kept back o let:
pſ. 21 w. 8. the Lord.	thine hand.
pſ. 145 w. 6. Jewen I.	moreover I.

The reſt, which have eſcaped through over-
ſight, you may amend, as you finde
them obvious.

Cliff leaned over her shoulder and read it. "I like that easygoing remark of his," said Cliff. " 'The rest you may amend as you find them obvious.' "

"And he did miss a few. But look at this particular one in the Preface of the Dodd, Mead facsimile—second line from the bottom, see? Where it says 'throughout the sciptures'?"

owne invētion; for which wee finde no warrant or
preſident in any ordinary officers of the Church
throughout the ſciptures.　Thirdly. Becauſe
the booke of pſalmes is ſo compleat a Syſtem of
　　　　　　　　　　　　　　　　pſalmes

"Daye missed that one," said Mona. "But look at the Winthrop copy—it's spelled *correctly* there, when it *should* have been a typo."

owne invētion; for which wee finde no warrant or prefident in any ordinary officers of the Church throughout the fcriptures.   Thirdly. Becaufe the booke of pfalmes is fo compleat a Syftem of pfalmes

"Oh, ho!" said Cliff. "Terrific, Mona! I wasn't expecting results this fast!" He hugged her shoulder.

"Watch it, there."

"Sorry. Got carried away."

"That's all right. I won't mind an end-of-the-job hug."

"You'll get one!"

"But does one inconsistency make the Winthrop copy a fake?"

Cliff frowned. "Not absolutely, but it certainly sets it apart from the other copies. . . . Or does it? Darn it, I suppose when you're finished we'll have to do a textual comparison with some of the other ones."

"Right. It could be that Stephen Daye noticed this type *after* he started his press run, corrected it, and went on with the printing. It would have been easy to do. Look how much space there is between 'sciptures' and 'Thirdly.' "

"That's true. Well, we'll just have to wait and see."

"But on second thought, I think the Winthrop copy *is* a fake."

"Why so?"

"Just a feeling. All the authors and proofreaders I've ever known simply go ape when they start finding typos in what is supposed to be camera-ready copy. They panic and start double-checking and triple-checking."

"And you don't think Daye did that?"

"I know he didn't. Not that he used a camera. Look at that

mistake on the very next page, at the end of the line halfway down, where it says 'extraordinary gifts.' Now, if Daye really cared enough about typos, he would have caught that one too; but if he *didn't* care about typos, why stop the press to put an 'r' in 'sciptures'? It doesn't make sense."

> **in Hezekiahs time, though doubtleſſe there were among them thoſe which had extraoridnary gifts to compile new ſongs on thoſe new ocaſions, as**

"No, it doesn't. So what's your theory?"

"That somebody was setting type for a fake book and accidentally spelled a word right."

"Which may be what Link Schofield discovered."

"However, I'll keep reading."

"Not today you won't," said Akira behind them. "It's five o'clock. I'm locking up the joint and heading for a sushi bar. Care to join me?"

"Why not?" said Cliff. "It's been months since I whiled away a quiet evening chewing on a strip of raw octopus."

"Tourist!"

EIGHT

Two mornings later, for reasons he didn't understand, waking up alone in the king-sized bed wasn't nearly as bad for Cliff as ordinarily. Most mornings, he left the bed as quickly as possible and avoided looking at the other side, unmussed, no dent in the pillow, no sound of running water in the shower, no quavering soprano rendition of Gilda's farewell song, *"Lassù in cielo vicina alla madre, in eterno per voi pregherò"*—to which Cliff often responded (off key) with Rigoletto's plea, *"No, lasciarmi non dei!"*

"You mustn't leave me . . ."

No tears this morning. "In fact, I feel good! Could it be that I'm starting to get over it? Well, never mind."

Making two trips from the kitchen, he carried his Tang, Spam and eggs, the coffee pot, the *Los Angeles Times,* and a wire reading rack out to the round table by the pool.

Winthrop had hit the front pages again in a long item that made breakfast hugely enjoyable. The reporter who wrote the story clearly had an equally good time with it. He had used, as a running theme, the currently popular "good news, bad news" jokes.

Winthrop had begun the day yesterday with some good news: The polls showed him leading the incumbent governor by 8 percentage points. In good spirits he had gone down to clamber over the cobblestones of Olvera Street to woo the Chicano vote. A photograph depicted him looking very much like the great Mexican singer Miguel Aceves Mejía, wearing a wide-brimmed charro's sombrero, black felt trimmed with silver braid (pushed well back on his head so his famous flashing smile would show).

The reporter also gleefully noted the first bit of bad news: For the photograph Winthrop thought it would be a good idea to pose with one of Olvera Street's red macaws perched on his hand, but when he approached the macaw the big bird bit him on the index finger, making a nasty gash. It must have hurt, but Winthrop won people's hearts by exclaiming, "Darn it, I was hoping *I'd* be the first one to draw blood in this campaign!"

He then made an impromptu speech from a flight of stone steps leading up to one of the shops on the slanting street. Reaction to the speech was mixed. The good news was that he won cheers by asserting that all Mexicans who had entered the country illegally to work on farms and in factories should be issued official permits and immunity against deportation, because they were obviously alleviating a shortage in such jobs. The bad news was that he stirred up loud protests by saying, in his peroration, "Therefore, California—and the federal government—should allow to remain, and even become citizens if they wish, any wetbacks who are already here."

Too late, his advisers informed him that the term "wetbacks" is considered pejorative, and that in the future he should refer to them as "undocumented aliens," or better still, learn a little Spanish and call them *indocumentados*.

But worse was to come. Winthrop had wanted to confine himself that day to issues of concern to Hispanic-Americans, but the reporters wouldn't let him. They were after hotter stuff. Acting like tackles for the Pittsburgh Steelers, they elbowed those issues aside and blitzed in to sack the quarterback. In particular, they hammered at him with questions on two recent developments in his campaign.

As one way for California to make up for the revenues it would lose by reducing taxes, Winthrop had suffested legalizing dog racing once again, but this time under the strict supervision of a racing commission "to keep corrupt criminal elements out of the sport." Perhaps it would be a good idea, too, to extend horse-racing seasons at the state's several tracks.

When the reporters chaffed him about his long-standing opposition to gambling and his vigorous prosecution of bookies, Winthrop replied with Emerson's observation that a foolish consistency is the hobgoblin of little minds. "Mind you, with my Puritan background I *am* opposed to gambling. But I am also a realist. I see Californians flocking to Las Vegas every weekend to gamble. If keeping some of that money at home will relieve the tax burden on working people who have to count the pennies, then I'm for it."

"Couldn't have put it better myself," said Cliff, taking a last forkful of basted egg and Spam before turning to page 6, Part IA.

"Mr. Winthrop," a reporter queried, "if you're opposed to gambling but want to keep gambling money in California, how do you reconcile that with your recent acquisition of a one-percent ownership in the Mirage Casino in Las Vegas? Or is that report true?"

Winthrop flashed a smile suggestive of a basking shark sidling up to a tuna.

"You fellas just won't leave me alone on that one, will you? You're worse than that macaw." (Laughter.) "Yes, the report is true. I plead guilty to investing money. But why do you say 'Mirage Casino'? The Mirage is a hotel, and yes—it does have a casino. So does the Hilton International Hotel and the MGM Grand. Like the late Conrad Hilton and Howard Hughes, yes—I have made an ordinary business investment in a hotel that has a casino. I need the money." (Laughter.)

"But Mr. Winthrop," put in a woman reporter in a loud and rasping voice, "do you really find it comfortable being a business associate of Tally Pellegrino?"

Winthrop had bristled. He knew what she was doing. The reporter, Velma Starkey, had almost won a Pulitzer Prize two years ago for an exposé of rapacious owners of retirement homes who plundered the estates of their helpless clients. She

was a crusader who had run out of crusades and was beating
the bushes for a new cause. She wanted that Pulitzer.

"Straining at a gnat, aren't you, Mrs. Starkey? If I buy stock
in Occidental Petroleum, does that make me a business associate of Armand Hammer?"

"Aren't those two different cases? You actually know Tally
Pellegrino, don't you?"

"Not well enough to call him 'Tally,' as you do."

A short paragraph informed nescient readers that Italo
"Tally" Pellegrino was manager of the Mirage Casino and
part owner of the Mirage Hotel; that the Internal Revenue
Service had twice grudgingly cleared him of skimming the
gambling take in the casino cage; and that the Nevada State
Gaming Commission, although its investigations revealed
that Pellegrino was "acquainted with" a distressing number
of figures in organized crime, could not honestly affirm that
he ever "consorted with" them.

"Exactly what do you have against Mr. Pellegrino, Mrs.
Starkey?"

Mrs. Starkey sputtered and gabbled for a moment.

"And as a lawyer, I would advise you to choose your words
very carefully indeed," he said with a pleasant smile.

"Well—he doesn't have a very good reputation, does he?"

"No. Neither did Jesus Christ and his disciples. (Laughter.)
And now, if you people will excuse me, I have other appoint-
ments."

Cliff folded the paper and put it aside. "And so ends another
tough day on the hustings. God, I'm glad I'm not a politician."

Hearing the familiar motor of the postman's three-wheeled,
red, white, and blue cart at the curb on Sunset Boulevard,
Cliff ambled out to the mailbox and was astonished to find a
letter from C. T. Post at Yale, one of the miracles of the Postal
Service being its ability to deliver mail from the East Coast to
Los Angeles in one day, whereas three or four days often
passed as a letter crawled from Santa Monica to Beverly
Hills, some ten miles away.

He went back to the table by the pool and slit the envelope.

Dear Clifford Dunbar:

From the sound of it, you are embarked on a very interesting project. Reading between the lines of your letter, I surmise that Lincoln Schofield had doubts about the book's authenticity, as you do, and that you suspect a possible connection between the book and his murder. I can't imagine what that connection could be, but if there is one, and if I had to choose between a black mark on my reputation as a scholar and apprehending Schofield's assailants, I would certainly opt for the latter and to hell with my pride. It was a disgusting crime.

If you're anything like me, you probably have, by now, learned more about the *Bay Psalm Book* than you really wanted to know, like the little girl who returned the book on penguins to the library. It *is* a wretched book, isn't it? It looks like something Penrod and Sam cranked out in the family stable. As I read through it—doggerel, meandering lines of print, weird spelling, and all—I kept expecting the name of Harold Ramorez to crop up as he shot people in the "abodmen." Penrod's prose was not much inferior to the verse in this book.

But to play devil's advocate as you requested— yes, several aspects of the book bothered both me and Silliman, not always equally, of course. Unfortunately, our misgivings could furnish only *negative* evidence at best for your purposes. Be that as it may, they were:

1. The absence of foxing (but that's fairly common).

2. The lack of any documentary provenance for the book—no mentions in correspondence, or in executors' inventories of the assets of various Winthrops' estates, etc.

3. The sudden appearance of a perfect copy. This bothered me more than it did Silliman. Consider-

ing the publicity the book has received over the past hundred years—especially the skyrocketing prices that copies have fetched on the few occasions when they've been on the auction block—wouldn't you think *somebody* in or connected with the Winthrop family would have let it be known before now that a superb eleventh copy existed? However, these things occur, as we see occasionally in the newspapers when a "long-lost masterpiece by Rembrandt" is discovered by a helpful granddaughter while she's tidying up Granny Cratchit's attic.

4. The size of the paper, and this is connected with the perfection of the Winthrop copy. If you have read up on the physical characteristics of the *Bay Psalm Book*, you may have been startled by the sharp variation in the size of the leaves. In one copy, for instance, the leaves are four and three-sixteenths of an inch wide; in another copy, they are four and three-quarters—over half an inch wider! In height, however, the leaves vary only from about six and fifteen-sixteenths to about seven and one-sixteenth. Most of the difference is due to shrinkage of the paper—to the extent that the printed lines in one particular copy are almost an eighth of an inch wider than in some of the others. This shrinkage results when the pages in one copy are exposed to the air more than those of another copy are—meaning that the book has been opened more often. Such pages are also more, shall we say, crinkly? than the smoother and flatter paper in less-used copies.

5. Now, the leaves in the Winthrop copy are pretty small: four and three-sixteenths wide by six and fifteen-sixteenths high. These figures imply that the book was exposed to the air a great deal—

that the book was used a great deal. Yet the leaves are smooth, the book is unmarked and not dog-eared, and no leaves are missing—features that are consistent with Perry Winthrop's statement that the book stood *neglected* on a shelf for many years.

6. But then if the book was untouched for so long, how come it needed rebinding? Oh, well—could happen. After all, only four copies have their original bindings. Calf gets pretty brittle with age, and somebody may have dropped the book on the floor.

And that's about it, Dr. Dunbar: a few peculiarities that gave me pause, but nothing to preclude my vouching for the book's authenticity (obviously, seeing that I *did* vouch for it).

I hesitate to wish you good luck—but good luck.

Best regards,
C. T. Post

The letter was much what he expected: Nothing to damn the book, of course, but Post's commentary on the puzzling shrinkage of the paper added one more serious indictment. If books could be bound over for trial, surely a jury would convict this one.

But the book was not on trial. Only solid, positive evidence would expose it, and that probably would have to come from Mona if it came at all. He was anxious to check back with her, but he decided to leave her alone for the morning so she could concentrate. He'd see her in the afternoon.

He devoted the rest of the morning to writing letters, including a thank-you note to C. T. Post, and taking care of the mechanical tasks of living that bored him out of his skull: a fill-'er-up at the gas station, a haircut, clothes at the cleaners, a bank deposit. As he lunched in a Westwood tearoom, he rewarded himself for his suffering by reading Scott Berg's biography of Maxwell Perkins.

After lunch he took his empty briefcase up to the English Department to clean out the last handful of books and papers that remained in his office. The bare room saddened him. It betokened the failure of an important enterprise. But as he went through the doorway he said to himself, "*Ave atque vale*, then," and, figuratively twitching his mantle blue, "tomorrow to fresh woods and pastures new."

He turned in his keys at the departmental office where Dorothy Stuart, the departmental secretary, sat alone minding the store.

"You're going to be missed around here, Clifford," she said in a languid tone that outsiders would have mistaken for indifference.

"Think so, Dorothy?"

"I know I'm going to miss you. And so will three hundred students and eight or ten faculty members. You were a breath of spring in this place. You woke people up."

Dr. Milton Phipps, the Renaissance specialist, came through the doorway at that moment, and seeing the keys lying on the counter, knew at once what was going on. Phipps was a very small man, about five feet three and slightly built, with the bright energy and quick movements of a terrier. He was an expert on Renaissance science and its influence on literature.

"About to leave us, Clifford?"

"That's right, Milt."

"May I ask what you plan to do with yourself?"

"I honestly have no idea."

"Would you possibly consider . . . reconsidering?"

"I didn't know there was anything to reconsider."

"Look, Clifford, I realize there's no love lost between you and Evan Brodhead."

"Cne might say that."

"And Evan does ride roughshod over people sometimes."

"I know. I still bear the hoofmarks."

"But I take over as department chairman in the fall, and

I'm sure the faculty can be swayed in your favor—especially in view of that brilliant article of yours in *PMLA*."

"I thought you were part of the opposition this spring."

"I was, and I was wrong."

"It was the article, mainly, that changed your mind?"

"Of course. You proved that you can do brilliant research. But how could we know? You're stubborn as hell, you realize."

"I know that."

"You refused to report on your research progress to Evan Brodhead, and then you came out and solved a problem that has baffled Chaucer scholars for a hundred years."

"I wasn't trying to be tricky, Milt."

"No, just stubborn as hell. And now look at the fine legacy you've stuck me with. Suddenly you're the talk of medieval scholars everywhere. Can you imagine what we're going to look like when they hear we *dropped* you from the *faculty*? They'll lump us right in with the rest of the lunatic fringe in Southern California."

"I'm sorry about that."

"Well, if we offered to renew your contract, would you be willing to let bygones be bygones and come back aboard?"

"Thanks, but no."

"Is tenure bothering you? If so, an associate professorship—"

"No, no, Milt, it isn't that at all. Milt, you once borrowed Mary McCarthy's *Memories of a Catholic Girlhood* from me. Remember that marvelous chapter where she wanted to shock everyone and call attention to herself in that Catholic girls' school, so she announced that she had 'lost her faith'? And then she was astounded to realize that she really had? Much the same thing happened to me at the end of April when I got angry and blurted out that I didn't even want to teach anymore. When I cooled off, I admitted I said that in the heat of anger, but then I realized I *meant* it."

"We all feel that way at times, Clifford: Wouldn't teaching

be wonderful if there were no students and no papers."

"You know why I became a medievalist, Milt? Because I'm good at languages and because when I was a kid I loved to read about Robin Hood and the Knights of the Round Table. Wouldn't it be terrific, I thought, if someday I could just read, read, read, and be paid for it?"

"That's how we all got started."

"I felt no urge whatever to teach, or do research."

"Of course not. What does a boy know about research?"

"Anyway, this you-can't-fire-me-I-quit situation is probably the best thing that ever happened to me. The big danger now is that having money may ruin me."

"I wish I had your problem. Is it correct to infer that you won't leave hating all of us?"

"Absolutely. Damn fools do occur on this faculty, but I'm right there among 'em. H. L. Mencken once said that every man, in his own way, is a damn fool, and I'm no exception."

"Nor am I, Clifford. Nor am I."

Cliff clapped him on the arm. "Maybe not, but you're a good man, Milt. Among other things, you're honest. *And* your book on alchemy in Renaissance literature is one of the best pieces of scholarship I ever read."

"Oh, get the hell out of here. Go spend some money."

"You'll come see us, won't you?" said Dorothy.

"Of course. And I'll be around a while anyway. I'm doing a final piece of bibliographic research."

"What on?" asked Phipps.

"I'm trying to find out who killed Link Schofield."

"What does bibliography have to do with it?"

"I'll let you know when I find out."

Cliff then made his official exit.

NINE

Cliff felt a twinge of disappointment when he walked into Special Collections and saw that Mona wasn't there. The intellectual girl with the horn-rimmed glasses and dandruff was still earthworming her way through the *Life of Wolsey*, and an attractive blond girl sat at the end of the room near one of the windows in the west wall, hunched over a reading rack. Otherwise the room was empty except for Akira.

An odd feeling seized Cliff. With a mild thrill that began in his groin and ran up to his chest, he realized that his main concern wasn't progress with the proofreading. *He wanted to see Mona.*

The pretty blonde at the end of the room looked up with a bright smile when she heard the glass-paned door shut behind Cliff. His heart bounded when he saw that it *was* Mona.

He moved down the aisle toward her, glad that it was a long room, long enough to give him time to recover his aplomb. She looked like a new person. Gone were the eucalyptus seedpod beads and scruffy clothes. She had washed her hair and possibly used a blond rinse, for the curls that clustered neatly around her head made him think of dandelions. She wore a fresh, white cotton, short-sleeved dress dotted with little yellow flowers, and a single strand of cultured pearls. The bodice of her dress was cut in a square yoke that revealed half an inch of cleavage. ("Just enough to let you know she's got 'em," Cliff reflected wryly, and then felt ashamed of himself.)

They beamed at each other.

"How's it going?"

"I found another one—maybe a clincher. But guess who dropped in on us today."

"Us?"

"Me and Mr. Yonenaka."

"Akira," said Akira, coming up behind Cliff.

"Me and Akira, then."

"Who did?"

"Our almost-governor."

"*Winthrop*? What was he doing here?"

"He said he'd just called on the chancellor," said Akira, "and so, as long as he was on the campus, why not drop in on the new home of the *Bay Psalm Book*—see if it's being put to profitable use, and so on."

"Uh-huh."

"So I said, with somewhat loud enthusiasm—"

"Thank God," said Mona. "Gave me time to whip up a story."

"I told him yon graduate student was deriving great profit therefrom. I didn't tell him Mona is a physical therapist."

"And he headed straight for me," said Mona. "I damn near widdled."

"Did he see what you were doing?"

"He *looked*, and he *asked* what I was doing. I told him I was doing an intercopy comparison of the two books as part of a study of American incunabula."

"And what did he say?"

"He wanted to know what incunabula are. 'The earliest printed books,' I said."

"Did he buy it?"

"Who could tell? Oh, he made some nice noises. 'Well, that's splendid, young lady! I'm pleased to see my little bequest being put to good use,' and all that—in that false-hearty manner of politicians."

"Did he see your notes?"

"Yes and no. I turned my cards over when he started down the aisle, but I had written '23rd Psalm' on the back of the last card. He may or may not have seen it."

"Was that your new discovery for the day?"

"Yes, and this one is too much. Wouldn't you say the Twenty-third Psalm is the best-known one?"

"Far and away."

"Well, take a look at the first line of the Dodd, Mead facsimile."

> ## 23   *A* Pſalme of David.
> ## THe Lord to mee a ſhepheard is,
> ##   want therefore ſhall not I.

"Gee, what rotten poetry!" said Akira.

"A *haiku* it isn't," Cliff agreed.

"Now look at the Winthrop copy."

> ## 23   *A* Pſalme of David.
> ## THe Lord to mee a ſhepherd is,
> ##   want therefore ſhall not I.

"Whoever set this type," Mona went on, "duplicated that funny spelling of 'mee' and then blew it by dropping the 'a' out of 'shepheard.' "

"Fascinating," said Cliff.

"The plot thickens," said Akira.

"The book *has* to be a forgery, right?"

"I'd certainly think so, Mona." Cliff frowned.

"Why the hesitation?"

"Well . . . Suppose discrepancies in spelling were all we found. That would mean, let's see—that this is an unknown second edition, or at least a slight variant of the first—*still* dated 1640, although the records don't show a second until 1651, when a revised and enlarged edition of two thousand copies came out."

"But what if," said Akira, "this one actually *preceded* the other known copies. That would make this book the sole survivor of a *true* first edition!"

"You two are going to have muscle spasms bending over so

far backward," said Mona. "Neither of those alternatives makes any sense at all."

"Why not?"

"They both imply that no matter which one came first, the printer later went through his locked-up chases of type and arbitrarily changed a word here, a word there. It isn't impossible, but it sure is ridiculous."

"You're right."

"However," Mona continued, "even if that's what Stephen Daye did, the Winthrop copy *still* has to be the later printing."

"How come?"

"The word 'scriptures' is spelled correctly in the Winthrop copy, but it's spelled 'sciptures' in the others. If the Winthrop copy came first, you can't tell me Stephen Daye would have deliberately pulled the 'r' out of there so the word would be misspelled from then on."

Cliff gazed at her in admiration. "My God, Mona, of course! If I'm that dumb, maybe it's just as well I'm getting out of teaching. And you ought to become a bibliographer!"

"No, thanks. I'll content myself with applying hot hydrocalators to the muscle spasms you two are asking for. Meanwhile, shall I go on with the proofreading?"

"By all means. Let's get a complete record of discrepancies and take it from there. We've already found enough to justify asking Silliman and Post to take another look. You're doing a sensational job, Mona."

She looked up at him with a green-eyed smile so charming that he wanted to kiss the tip of her nose. But he restrained himself.

"I think I'd better make a couple of phone calls. Mind if I use your phone, Akira?"

"Sure, but no toll calls, okay? Use the phone in Link's office."

He sat down in Link's chair, consulted the campus phone directory, and asked for extension 405.

"Chancellor's office."

"This is John Skelton of the *Los Angeles Times*. I'm phoning from Westwood. Is Perry Winthrop still with the chancellor, or am I too late to get a story?"

"I beg your pardon. There must be some mistake. Mr. Winthrop hasn't been here today, and the chancellor went to Santa Barbara this morning."

"Another case of crossed wires. Sorry to bother you."

"Not at all. You might try the chancellor's residence."

"Thank you, I will."

He phoned the chancellor's residence. The chancellor's wife answered the phone and informed him that the chancellor had not returned from Santa Barbara.

"Ah, *ha!*" Cliff exclaimed, whirling in the swivel chair.

"Plot still thickening?" Akira called from his office.

"It's still only three-finger poi, but it's getting there."

He stepped outside the office and beckoned to Mona.

"Winthrop was lying. He didn't visit the chancellor."

"Which means he came straight here to see what was going on."

"Which means he's worried," said Akira.

"Which means the book has to be a forgery," said Mona.

"But do you think he's connected in some way with Link's murder?" asked Akira.

"Oh, no. Certainly not directly. The man's an ambitious politician, yes, maybe even ruthless, but murder? That's a little too Soviet Union for me."

"It doesn't seem to fit his character."

"I would also feel more sure of myself if we could find a Nixon-type smoking pistol that would condemn this book once and for all. Something blatant that no jury could misconstrue. Because I am now convinced that the book and the murder truly are connected somehow."

"Maybe Winthrop *arranged* to have Link killed. A hired assassin."

"Still out of character."

"Then we're back where we started."

"That's enough for a Friday afternoon," said Akira. "Let's shut up shop and go home." He went back into his office to lock things up.

"I guess that's it for the day," said Mona. She looked at Cliff brightly but didn't turn to go because she saw that he was staring at her, either thoughtfully or vacantly.

The westering sun, as if on cue from a lighting director, had darted a first sheaf of yellow rays beneath the half-lowered venetian blinds and onto the left half of Mona's face. A mist of tiny golden hairs glowed along her cheekline; one green eye glowed like an emerald.

"Uh, Mona," Cliff began. He rubbed his scar and ran his hand down his back hair. "If you're not already doing something tonight, I thought we might have dinner and maybe see a movie. There's a new Jean-Luc Godard film playing in the village. . . . We could bone up on our French," he added with a laugh that came out more like a cackle.

Holy smoke, I sounded like a tenth-grader! he thought. I *feel* like a tenth-grader! But I'm out of practice.

"Oh, darn! I'm sorry, Cliff. I have a date I made several days ago and I can't break it."

"Quite all right! I didn't give you much notice."

"How about tomorrow night?" she said. "Are *you* free?"

My God, she's charming! he thought.

"Thank you," he said.

"For what?"

"For one of the smoothest examples of helping a guy save face I ever heard."

"Well, are you?"

"Am I what?"

"Free, dummy."

"Yes, Yes, I am. Free. How about if I pick you up at seven? And maybe I'll think of something better than a movie."

"Fine, but keep a curb on your imagination."

"*Miss—Moore!*"

TEN

*T*o avoid sitting at home alone, struggling to read a book while wondering what sort of guy Mona had a date with—no doubt some bearded education major who insisted that teachers should be called "change agents"—he went to the movies by himself.

Both films in the double feature included what now appear to be obligatory sex scenes, in which the principal characters get to take their clothes off and writhe about in the raw with much clutching and heavy breathing through the nose. The scenes irritated Cliff; they did nothing to advance the plot, and they aroused him sexually in spite of himself, with the result that he left the theater before the second feature was over, feeling simultaneously angry and raunchy.

It was a little after midnight when he approached his Porsche at the far end of an asphalt parking lot, in a corner formed by the rear brick walls of a dry cleaner's and a bookstore.

Both of the young men who stepped out to meet him carried open switchblades. One of the men sidled around to Cliff's rear.

Instant spasm of fear. Instant surge of adrenaline and trembling muscles.

"Hey, teach! Let's have the billfold!"

Cliff shifted to an angle where he could see both of them. The leader seemed to be the one who spoke—the gaunt, pale-faced one with the straggly goatee. The black-haired one with the fat lower lip was the backup.

Cliff looked quickly to see how they held their knives.

Amateurs, both of them. They held their knives in their fists, for stabbing. That helped. When your opponent holds his knife between thumb and fingers, ready for slashing, the wise thing to do is start running like a jackrabbit.

Goatee flipped his left hand in a beckoning gesture and said, "Come on, the billfold!"

Old trick. As Cliff reached inside his jacket for the billfold, Fat Lip would hit him from the rear.

Goatee took an impatient step forward.

Cliff dropped to the pavement on his left side, hooked his left foot behind Goatee's forward ankle to hold his leg in place, and kicked Goatee's knee as hard as he could. The knee joint popped loudly and Goatee went down, crippled and howling, as Cliff rolled to his left and onto his feet to meet the onrushing Fat Lip.

With his forearm, Cliff blocked the knife hand as it came down, but not before the knife point dug into his wrist. At the same time, he lifted his knee into Fat Lip's crotch. The knee didn't land solidly, but in twisting to avoid it, Fat Lip went off balance.

Cliff seized him by the shirtfront with both hands and flung himself backward, still holding on. When his back met the asphalt he placed both feet in Fat Lip's belly and pushed hard. Fat Lip's legs went straight up in the air over his head, and there he hung suspended upside down, as if the two of them were performing a fancy stunt for tumblers.

Cliff had perhaps one and one-half seconds to decide: He could let go, in which case Fat Lip would fly through the air, crash, and skid twenty feet or so, or he could hold on, yank down, and smash Fat Lip's skull on the pavement.

Cliff held on. His killer instinct, still lingering from combat, very nearly overwhelmed him. But at three quarters of a second, he relaxed his grip and merely let Fat Lip's head bang onto the asphalt. Fat Lip collapsed with a thud.

Cliff rose to his feet, trembling, dirty, besmeared with road oil. He bound his handkerchief around his wrist to stop the bleeding.

Goatee had pushed himself backward against the brick wall and managed to ease himself up to a standing position on one leg.

"God damn! God damn! God damn!"

Cliff snatched up a knife and held the point under Goatee's chin.

"Okay, who hired you to do this?"

"Son-of-a-bitch! Broke my fuckin' leg!"

Cliff stuck the knife an eighth of an inch into Goatee's flesh. Blood trickled down the blade.

"I said, who hired you?"

Goatee's eyes bulged downward.

"Nobody! This was just a heist!"

Cliff stuck in the knife a trifle more.

"Who?"

"I don't know who he was! Never saw him before!"

"Where?"

"Silver Slipper in Palms!"

"What's he look like?"

"Middle-aged dude. Gray crewcut. Tan corduroy jacket."

"Fat or skinny?"

"Uh—fat."

"What's his name?"

"I tell ya I don't know!"

"How much did he pay you?"

Desperate eyes. Trying to weigh choices.

"I think your pal has a fractured skull, man, and I'd just as soon make it a pair. What did he pay you?"

"A grand now. Four grand afterward."

"When?"

"Next Tuesday night."

"What's your name?"

Pause. Hell. Name's on driver's license. "Bruce Flett."

"What's your pal's name?"

"Peasoup Richardson."

"Ever kill anybody before? Did you kill a man named Lincoln Schofield?"

"Hell, no! What kind of trip you tryin' to lay on me?"

"Okay, Bruce. Relax." He withdrew the knife.

"Relax! Get me to a hospital, man! Fuckin' leg's killin' me!"

"I'll get the cops. They'll take care of you."

You don't have to wait long for a black-and-white in Westwood on a weekend night. Officer Carruthers, forty-three and white, and Officer Layton, twenty-three and black, both of them spic and span in sharply creased blues, were startled at the small battlefield scene.

"You're an *English* professor, Dr. Dunbar?"

"That's right."

"Christ, you certainly cried havoc and let slip the dogs of war, didn't you?"

Cliff smiled wanly.

"Surprised you, huh? I got tired of reading Wonder Woman comics and went to the other extreme," said Carruthers. "I like the Bard's dialog better. Well, let's check out the *dramatis personae* here." He shined his flashlight in Goatee's face. "You don't look so good, citizen."

"Son-of-a-bitch broke my fuckin' leg!"

"This one?" Carruthers rapped his flashlight on Goatee's disjointed knee. Goatee clenched his teeth and grunted.

"Fuckin' pig!"

"Ah, ah! Manners!" Carruthers rapped him on the head sharply. "Well, I suppose I should call for a police ambulance. Goes against the grain, but I guess you could call it good community relations."

"I'd say the suspect lying on the ground needs a hearse," said Officer Layton.

"Naw, he's still breathin'," said Carruthers.

"I'm very sorry about that," said Cliff. "I didn't need to hurt him that badly."

"Didn't *need* to?"

"I could just have scuffed him up."

"Hell, I think you did him a favor," said Carruthers. "He'll probably give up crime and enroll in divinity school."

"Let's hope so."

"This being assault with a deadly weapon, though, I'll have to ask you to come down to the West L.A. Division and file a report. Know where it is, over on Butler in Sawtelle? Good. But stay here till the ambulance comes, and I'll write up my own report."

"Hey—officer," said Goatee. "How about lettin' me sit down?"

"Certainly." Layton opened the rear door of the black-and-white. "Hop in," he said with a malicious grin.

On his way to the police station, Cliff stopped at a drive-in restaurant, washed up a bit, and made phone calls to Mona and Akira Yonenaka. Mona's phone rang ten times, but nobody answered. Her roommate was out, too. That worried him somewhat, but he assumed Mona was still out on her date. Akira answered the phone on the first ring, and Cliff gave him a rundown on the assault and on his suspicions.

"To be on the safe side, Akira, make sure your door's locked and don't go anywhere tonight."

"Who's going anywhere at one in the morning?"

"One never knows."

"What do you think I am, one of those *ninja*? But thanks for the warning. Maybe I'll move in with my father for a day or two. You're really okay, Cliff?"

"Oh, a small scratch. But no doubt about it, I've got a tiger by the tail now."

"And there's an Oriental saying that the man who rides the tiger is afraid to get off. Watch your step."

The drive to the West L.A. Division gave Cliff time to calm down and analyze, and decide exactly what to tell the police. He had no doubt at all now that there were connections among this assault, Link's murder, and the *Bay Psalm Book*— and evidently in some way, however tenuous, with Winthrop's campaign; but it would wreck everything to spill all this to the police now. It would merely cause all the dogs to lie low, deny everything, slam doors, plug leads, and do nothing suspicious.

To keep quiet was the wisest course, but it would involve an ill-smelling slurry of lies, small truths, and evasions, and he hated it. Lie to the police? What had become of that model citizen and man of principle who defied faculty committees and was supposed to be a model for his students?

The West L.A. station looked like a Montessori school on the outside and a reform school on the inside: bare scuffed walls, asphalt tile, benches, and a long, black-topped counter, behind which two bored policemen operated their paper mill.

Two drunk-and-disorderlies were brought in after a bar fight, reeling and roaring about their civil rights, which apparently included vomiting on each other. A humiliated father from an upper-crust family was bailing out his teenage son—something about three outstanding warrants and no registration on a Baja Bug—while trying to impress the police officers with his good breeding, excellent English, and impending candidacy for sainthood.

Officers Carruthers and Layton had checked back into the station. Layton led him down a hall to Lieutenant Puterbaugh's office, a bleak room full of paper and filing cabinets, with dusty blinds, dusty desk, dusty typewriter. The only personal touch Cliff could see was a bowling trophy atop a filing cabinet, on which a golden bowler, ball swung to the rear, was frozen forever in midstride like a figure on Keats' Grecian urn. "Forever shalt thou bowl, and she keep score . . ."

Lieutenant Puterbaugh, in shirt sleeves, sat embedded in paper, looking discouraged. He shook hands perfunctorily with Cliff and invited him to sit down, then rolled a form sheet into his typewriter and began asking routine questions: name, address, phone, age, occupation.

Cliff watched him with interest. The lieutenant was a fast typist in spite of looking like a former noseguard for the Rams. Puterbaugh had a bald head, black hair much like a monk's tonsure, beefy shoulders, eyes like black coals.

"A professor of English? Where did you learn to be a one-man earthquake—Harvard?"

Cliff laughed. "I was a combat officer in Vietnam. We had a lot of hand-to-hand combat training."

"Yeah, I can tell. Now, these two punks who went for you. Got any idea why they singled you out in particular?"

"No. I'm not even sure they did."

"It looks to me like they did. They either followed you out of the theater or they were waiting for you at your car, one or the other."

"I hadn't thought of that."

"So why pick on you? Punks like that usually go for women, gays, old men, little guys, whatever. Did you have a lot of money on you they could have seen in your billfold when you bought your ticket?"

"No. Thirty or forty dollars."

"Then why you? You're a tall, well-built guy and you don't wear a sign around your neck that says 'English teacher.' "

"I don't know—unless they felt confident because the parking lot was deserted. I was alone, and there were two of them."

"Yeah, could be. Still sounds fishy, though. You have any enemies?"

"A few English teachers, but they aren't the kind you're thinking of."

"Any who would want to do you in?"

"They already have done me in—that is, they fired me, and I resigned. Their idea of violence is to deny tenure."

"You're leaving the faculty?"

"Yes, in ten days or so I'll be a civilian again."

"But you'll still be at this address?"

"Yes."

"Okay, then, you'll be notified when these characters come up for arraignment and trial. You'll be called on to testify."

"Fine."

"Anything more you want to add?" Alert, questioning glance.

"No, not a thing. Maybe one suggestion."

"Yeah?"

"This is a long shot, of course, but you might want to really grill this Bruce Flett to see if he had anything to do with the murder of Lincoln Schofield a few weeks ago. He was a librarian at LAU and he was—"

"I know who he was. That's one of my cases."

"Oh! Then you must know his daughter, Pearl Humphrey."

"I know her. She calls me every couple of days. So what's the connection with your case?"

"I just thought—well, Link was a friend of mine, and maybe it's merely coincidence, but we were both attacked at night in Westwood by two guys with knives."

"There's a lot of knives in Los Angeles, Dr. Dunbar. There's even a lot of knives in Westwood. We also have an eyewitness who was on the scene and saw two *black* dudes leaving Schofield's garage."

"I know. But she could have been mistaken."

"How did you know it was a she?"

"Pearl Humphrey told me. And it was in the papers."

"Sure."

"Check into it, will you?"

"I'll check into it. The case is still open." Puterbaugh fixed steady eyes on him. "You'll excuse me, Dr. Dunbar, but I've got a feeling you know more than you're telling me."

"Oh—no. Maybe my imagination is running away with me."

Pregnant pause.

"All right, but think it over. If anything else occurs to you, give me a call. Here's my card."

Cliff took it, thanked him, and left with a feeling of relief and a great deal more respect for Los Angeles detectives than he had when he came in. Puterbaugh was anything but a B-movie gumshoe, and if he interviewed Flett in the prison ward of L.A. County Hospital, and if Flett admitted he'd been hired to kill Cliff, Puterbaugh was not going to be happy when he started investigating motives. It would be wise for Cliff to solve this case before they arrested him for withholding evidence.

Since Mona's apartment was only fifteen minutes away, he drove there directly instead of phoning. The building, on a quiet street west of the LAU campus, was a rabbit warren of a place, sliced and diced into tiny apartments for students, who paid exorbitant rent.

He was about to press the bell of her first-floor-rear apartment when Mona came down the hall with her date, who did not have a beard or wear glasses. He was handsome and athletic-looking in his tobacco-brown ultrasuede jacket, and he moved with the easy grace of a basketball player, which conceivably he could have been had he not been a runt who didn't top six-feet-two.

The date was taken aback and turned rather stiff at seeing a seedy bum with a bandage on his wrist about to press Mona's doorbell at two in the morning.

Mona's reaction was more forthright. Her face clouded over until she resembled Mount St. Helens spitting on its hands and getting ready to do a number on the Toutle River.

"Cliff—Dr. Dunbar—what is this?"

"I need to talk to you. It's urgent."

"So I see."

"You know this dude?" asked the date.

"I know him."

"Is he bothering you?"

"Not yet."

"Need any help?"

"No, I'll handle this."

"Listen, Mona, I'm sorry—I know this is a hell of a time but, ah, something's come up and, ah, oh, I suppose it *could* wait till morning."

"It *is* morning."

"I mean, like—you know, daylight." (Good God, I mark students down for using English like this! he thought.) "I certainly don't want to interrupt, or interfere . . ."

"I think you'd better stop talking. Rog, thanks for a terrific evening. Let's do it again, okay?"

"Okay. You sure you'll be all right?"

"I'm sure. Don't worry. Good night, Rog."

She gave him a quick kiss on the cheek and he ambled down the hall, glancing over his shoulder a time or two, puzzled.

"All right, what's the idea?"

"Listen, I tried to phone you."

"That, too?"

"Don't be angry."

"Well, I *am* angry! What do you expect?"

"Mona—hold it, or you're going to be embarrassed as hell. Two guys attacked me tonight in a parking lot."

"Attacked you?"

"With knives. They wanted to kill me. They were hired to."

"My God!"

He gave her a detailed account of the evening's fun, including his evasive interview with Lieutenant Puterbaugh.

"I feel rotten, though, over fracturing that thug's skull."

"You had no choice, did you?"

"I had a choice when I was holding him upside down in the air. My superego said 'no, no' and my id said 'yes, yes,' and my id won. I came within a hair of deliberately killing him."

"Well, he's a would-be murderer himself."

"Yes, but what about me?" The idea of killing makes me sick. I thought I left all that behind me in 'Nam. I thought I had risen above it. And yet when I faced the choice again, I nearly chose killing. I'd better reexamine myself. Maybe it'll make me have better control next time."

"Let's hope there won't be one."

"I'm afraid there will be. That's why I'm here."

"I don't follow you."

"I'm afraid they might come after *you*. Or Akira."

"Oh."

"Mona, I can't tell you how sorry I am to have involved you in this. Maybe you'd better bow out fast—go home to Oregon for the summer."

"No."

"That's a quick answer. Why?"

"I don't know. Maybe there is no why."

"But it's ludicrous, the idea of a proofreader being in danger for her life! I can't have you getting killed over a couple of typos, for God's sake!"

"I'm not going." She smiled puckishly. "I don't want to pass up all that money, and the job's interesting."

"In that event, I think you'd be safer to move in with me for the time being."

"Uh-huh."

"No, Mona, I'm serious."

"You mean right now?"

"Now. Pack a few things and let's go."

She took a blue vinyl suitcase from a closet shelf and went into her bedroom with it. He was interested in seeing where she lived. It was the cleanest student's apartment he had ever seen, certainly cleaner than his own room when he was in college. There were also the touching signs of student poverty and pluck: bookshelves consisting of boards resting on bricks; a dressing table made of a board resting on two upended orange crates with ruffled fabric thumbtacked over the openings; unframed prints scotch-taped to the walls. Escher, Manet. A too-expensive but necessary record player and tape deck. Half the books were dense-looking textbooks: *Introduction to . . . , Fundamentals of . . . , Advanced Techniques in . . .* anatomy, physical therapy, pharmacology. Many of the books were "good" books: Dostoevski, Bellow, Hemingway, Camus. Many others were written by Cliff's favorite mystery writers: Margery Allingham, Josephine Tey, P. D. James, Dorothy Sayers, Sjöwall, and Wahlöö.

"I apologize for getting so mad at you," Mona called from the other room.

"It's all right, we're even. I got mad at you, too."

"*You* got mad at *me*?"

"What do you think? You were assuming I wanted . . . that I was some sort of overheated adolescent."

"You'll have to admit that's what it looked like. And poor Roger! He didn't know you from Adam, so of course he assumed you're—interested in me."

"Maybe Roger's right."

"Good. A girl always appreciates interest. However, Cliff, my moving into your house doesn't necessarily mean there's going to be any hanky-panky."

"Hanky-panky?"

"Rannygazoo."

"Necessarily?"

"You heard me."

She appeared with her suitcase. "I left a note for Clara on the mirror. Let's go."

They hurried out to his Porsche and drove north on Veteran up to Sunset Boulevard. Mona was thoughtful.

"Cliff, how can you be certain those two thugs were after you personally?"

"The Flett character admitted they were hired."

"He could have made that up as an excuse. He'd have said anything with a knife at his throat."

"No, he knew who I was."

"How can you be sure?"

"He called me 'teach.' "

"Oh."

ELEVEN

*M*ona came out to the kitchen at ten the next morning, crisp in a mint-green skirt, white cotton blouse, and a necklace of round yellow beads.

"Your house is beautiful!"

"Thanks. I love it here. And good morning!"

He turned to look at her from the stove, where he was frying Canadian bacon and eggs. Again, she reminded him of a daisy.

"You look like springtime. *'Sur toutes les fleurs, j'aime la marguerite.'* "

"That's pretty. What is it?"

"A poem Chaucer liked—and used. There was a literary cult of the daisy in his time. Nobody knows how it got started, but the poets had a lot of fun with it." The toaster pinged. "Butter the toast, will you?"

"Sure. How long have you been up?"

"Couple of hours."

"You couldn't sleep?"

"I slept okay but I had phone calls to make." With a spatula he put the bacon onto a plate lined with paper towels.

"About what happened?"

"As a result of it. I'm having iron bars put over all the windows, in case of intruders, with quick-release mechanisms inside, in case of fire. And I'm having an electrically controlled iron gate put into that recessed entryway at my front door. They're coming out today."

"How did you get them to come on Saturday?"

"Money. I agreed to pay fifty percent more if they'd start today and finish the job over the weekend."

He slid basted eggs onto their plates. "Hope you like them this way."

"Perfect. And what timing! How did you know I was up?"

"Heard the shower. Let's have breakfast outside, okay? You bring the coffee pot."

She held the door open for him as he passed through with a tray. They sat down at the round table under a large umbrella near the pool.

"I can't believe the flowers back here! It looks like the county aboretum! What are those red ones that look like zinnias but aren't?"

"*Those* are daisies. Transvaal daisies. They're terrific. They love hot weather and sun and they bloom almost all year round."

"You must be quite a gardener."

"Me? Oh, no. All of that was—Carole's work."

"Your wife?"

"Yes."

"You loved her very much, didn't you?"

"Yes."

"That's good."

"Why so?"

"Means you're healthy. So you'll still be a decent prospect for some lucky girl."

"Your eggs are getting cold."

They concentrated on breakfast for several minutes of silence broken only by the whir of the wings of two hummingbirds who were breakfasting on hollyhocks and the scarlet hanging blooms of a bottlebrush tree.

"You've been living here alone for a year?"

"Mm-hm."

"What do you do for sex?"

His fork paused in midlift. "What? Oh—well—uh—"

She laid her fork down and slapped her forehead. "There I go again! You and your dumb big mouth, Mona Louise!"

"No, it's all right. Given the times we're living in, it's a natural enough question, I suppose."

"Do me a favor and forget I asked."

"I don't mind. The answer is—nothing. I simply lost all interest, to tell you the truth."

"Not permanently, I hope."

"I shouldn't think so. How about you? Ever been married?"

"Nope. Thought about it once."

"What happened?"

"*He* didn't think about it. He was getting all the benefits of marriage without any of the obligations, so why spoil a nice deal?"

"That's called being modern."

"Right. Our relationship was about as stable as the one between that hummingbird and the hollyhock."

"He dropped in when he needed nectar?"

"Right. Mind you, I'm all for the new feminism, at least the part that means equal opportunity and the right to be free and natural—about sex, for instance—but too many guys think it means they're free to move in, borrow money, forget to pay it back, forget to pay their half of the rent, up you and down you, drink your beer, and saunter off whistling 'God Save the Queen.' "

"Why, Mona! You're describing a meaningful relationship."

"Yes, and I know what the meaning is. No more, thanks. I shouldn't be too hard on him, though. He was a struggling musician and he did have to move around a lot. He was the most charming parasite I ever knew."

"Was this up in Oregon?"

"Yes."

"Will you be going back there?"

"In one more year, when I get my master's. I'll either go to work in a hospital or maybe with an orthopedic surgeon or a medical group."

"Sounds good. It's refreshing to meet someone who knows exactly what she wants to do."

"Oh, I'm Mona the realist. If I get married, I'll probably want to work. If I don't get married, I *know* I'll have to work. And with the divorce rate pushing fifty percent, I think every

woman should know how to do something that pays. Besides,
I like physical therapy."

"It seems to have done you a lot of good, too, I've noticed."

"Wait'll you see me in a bathing suit. Is your pool heated?"

"I turned it on this morning. It'll be okay tomorrow."

"I'll go in if you do."

"You're on. In the meantime, I'd better get moving."

"Where are you off to?"

"I'm going to drop in on Winthrop's campaign headquarters and try to see him."

"To sort of rattle his cage?"

"Exactly. You should be all right as long as you stick close
to home, and the workmen will be here. But just in case, do
you know how to handle a pistol? Work the safety and so on?"

"Yes, but I'd rather not. I've got Mace, and I'm licensed."

"Keep it handy."

He got up and started putting their dishes on the tray.

"I'll wash up," said Mona. "You go beard your lion."

It was not difficult to find Winthrop's headquarters on
Westwood Boulevard south of Wilshire. On the contrary, it
was hard to miss the gaudy red, white, and blue splash of
American flags, bunting, and campaign posters that con-
verted the front of a former grocery market into a Fourth of
July celebration. "Vote for Winthrop—the New Broom," the
posters urged. "A Clean Sweep with Winthrop."

Inside, the place hummed with the power of the American
political process, solidly based on paper, yellow pencils, tele-
phones, people's voices, and bulletin boards covered with
charts and schedules. A dozen volunteer women sat at a
dozen desks. All of them wore little plastic brooms labeled
"Winthrop" pinned to their blouses.

A very pretty girl with long brown hair and blue eyes, in a
smartly tailored suit, sat at a desk just inside the front
doorway. The desk was covered with neat stacks of campaign
literature and a box full of the plastic brooms.

"Good *morning!*" she said with a smile that outdazzled Winthrop's. "Can I *help* you?"

"I was hoping to see Mr. Winthrop if he's in."

"*Oh. Well*—" She glanced toward the back of the room. "His office is in the *rear* . . ." she said with a frown that registered both extreme doubt and sweet regret.

"Thanks. I'll give it a try."

"Meanwhile, take one of our packets—and let me pin this on you." With a double-dimpled smile, she pinned a broom to his lapel. "Who knows? Maybe it'll get you in."

He proceeded to an area at the rear surrounded by a low railing with a gate in it. At a desk behind the gate sat another woman, also attired in a tailored suit, but she was not smiling. Her black hair was pulled back in a bun, and her long, carmine fingernails and carmine lips would have convinced any passerby that this was one of Darwin's fittest. "Nature red in tooth and claw," as Tennyson put it.

"May I help you," she stated in a tone that meant no.

"I'd like to see Mr. Winthrop."

"Do you have an appointment?"

"No. I thought I'd just take a chance."

"I'm afraid Mr. Winthrop won't have a spare moment today."

"I believe he'll want to see me."

"Oh? And what is your name, please?"

"Dr. Clifford Dunbar. I'm on the staff at LAU."

"And what is the nature of your business?"

"It's rather personal—but tell him it's on the same subject that Lincoln Schofield once came to see him about."

Her finger moved toward a switch on her intercom; then she thought better of it and knocked perfunctorily on the office door and disappeared inside.

While she was gone, Cliff played a sort of matrix game with himself: If Winthrop refuses to see me, he's probably clean. If he lets me in immediately, he's probably guilty as hell about something. If he makes me wait only fifteen minutes, he's probably involved somehow but has to pretend ignorance. If he makes me wait thirty mintues, he's probably not involved but wants to be courteous. But what did Winthrop's own matrix look like?

As Cliff pursued this interesting thought, the woman came back. Inasmuch as she wore a faint smile, he surmised that she bore tidings of great joy.

"If you will kindly be seated, Mr. Winthrop will see you as soon as he's free."

"Thank you." He glanced at his watch. Ten minutes to eleven. To pass the time away, Cliff opened the campaign packet and began reading. As usual with campaign literature, its informational content was scanty. It merely left the reader with the impression that Winthrop embodied the more attractive qualities of Captain Miles Standish, Theodore Roosevelt, Andrew Carnegie, Art Linkletter, Audie Murphy, Saint Bernard of Clairvaux, and, to judge from the group photograph taken in front of a peeled-log fishing lodge, the Swiss Family Robinson. Cliff stuffed the leaflets back in their envelope and took out his thin volume of *Sir Gawain and the Green Knight*, edited by J. R. R. Tolkien. . . .

"Mr. Winthrop will see you now."

"Thank you."

He glanced at his wristwatch before he went through the doorway. Twelve minutes past eleven. He smiled. So much for the matrix.

Winthrop rose from behind his desk and came forward to meet him with outstretched hand and a warm smile.

"Delighted to see you again, Dr. Dunbar! Sorry to keep you waiting."

"Not at all. It's good of you to make time for me."

"Mrs. Roscommon tells me your visit has something to do with Lincoln Schofield." A painful frown clouded his face. "Dr. Dunbar, I simply cannot *express* how distressed I was over his murder. It was a terrible thing! He was such a fine old fellow, and absolutely one of a kind!"

Cliff was surprised to see that the pain on the man's face was genuine beyond a doubt. The realization rattled him.

"Yes, he was. A genuine scholar and a good friend."

They exchanged a few elegies to Link's memory, and Winthrop commented, "So I felt surprised and a little flattered when he showed up here that day."

"The day he was murdered?"

"As I remember, yes. Or was it the day before?"

"Was it morning or afternoon?"

"I can't recall—which is quite understandable, what with people coming and going all day here."

"Of course. What did he want to see you about?"

Damn it! I didn't mean to say that! he thought.

Winthrop gave him a sharp look. "You mean you don't know? Mrs. Roscommon gave me to understand you wanted to discuss 'the same subject.' "

"Well—yes." Might as well take the plunge. "The *Bay Psalm Book*."

"Of course," said Winthrop.

Cliff felt the thrill of unexpected victory.

"But I'm afraid," continued Winthrop, "that I'll have to give you the same answer I gave Schofield. I believe I have made a sufficient contribution by donating the book. My campaign expenses are so heavy that I can't afford to sponsor the project he had in mind. And besides, it would be more appropriate, it seems to me, for the university to supply the necessary funding."

"I don't understand. What project?"

"Reprinting the *Bay Psalm Book*."

Seeing the astonishment on Cliff's face, Winthrop gave a short laugh and said, "We seem to be talking at cross-purposes, Dr. Dunbar. Evidently Schofield didn't take you into his confidence. He pointed out to me that the book hasn't been reprinted since a very small edition back around 1900—and that one was a composite of several defective copies. He believed it would be a contribution to scholarship to reprint the perfect Winthrop copy in a substantial edition—a collo-type facsimile, I believe he called it—so it would be widely available. Most people don't even know what the book looks like. He also suggested to me—and quite right he was, too—that it would be excellent publicity for me and my campaign. I could pass out free copies, and so on. Appealing as the idea was, though, I had to turn it down. I couldn't afford it."

Cliff stared at him in wonderment.

"What's puzzling you, Dr. Dunbar?"

"I find that hard to believe."

"I don't know why. Surely you understand my position."

"No, no, I don't mean the money. I mean I find the whole proposition incredible. Link had nothing but contempt for the *Bay Psalm Book*!"

"Contempt? For a book worth a third of a million?"

"He thought it was a lousy book, which it is. It's a rotten book. It's a mere curio."

"Be that as it may, it's a very famous book and highly prized."

"Not by Link. I simply cannot imagine his wanting you to finance reprinting it."

"Well, there's not much I can do to repair your lack of imagination, is there?" (Teeth, featuring incisors.)

"Why do you suppose he brought the book with him?"

"I have no idea," said Winthrop. "It certainly wasn't neces-sary. I don't need to reexamine a book I've known since I was a toddler."

Cliff let that one pass.

"But you've got something else on your mind, haven't you? Why not come out with it if you have?"

Hesitantly, picking his words, Cliff replied, "I have reason to believe that Link suspected the book's authenticity. In which case . . . is it possible he brought the book to show you certain—shall we say, inconsistencies? Possibly to allow you to retract your donation and save face?"

"I withdraw my comment on your lack of imagination.

Colorful is scarcely the word for it! Let me remind you that the two foremost experts in the country have vouched for it."

"Experts have been known to make mistakes."

"Whose opinions would you prefer, then? Amateurs'? Such as your own and that of the young lady in the library? That's what you two are doing, isn't it? You assumed the book is counterfeit and you deliberately set out to prove it."

"No, the other way around. We started with a hypothesis and we're trying to see whether it's right or wrong."

"That's too hairsplitting for me. But you'd be pleased as Punch to prove the experts wrong, wouldn't you? Oh, don't bother with scholarly arguments, Dr. Dunbar. I see pretty clearly now who you are and what you represent. I am well aware that there is a large faction, probably a majority, in the university system who would like to see me defeated because I don't propose to inflate their budget twenty percent every year, or because I don't have a degree in minor art forms of the Post-King Tut Period or whatever. Anybody who doesn't give you a twenty-percent raise is by definition anti-intellectual, isn't that about the size of it?"

"Not as far as I'm concerned. In a few days I won't even be a faculty member any longer."

"Then what is your interest, if I may ask?"

"Mainly, I'm interested in finding out who murdered Link Schofield. He was my friend."

Winthrop turned and walked over to a window, where he stood gazing out in thought, his right hand in his pocket, idly jingling his small change. Turning, he said, "I have extremely mixed feelings about you, Dr. Dunbar. On the one hand, I wish you all the luck in the world in bringing the thugs who killed your friend to justice. I'll even donate money to that cause if it will help any. In that respect, I'm your champion and I have nothing but admiration for you. On the other hand, I want to give you a piece of ice-cold advice: As it said on the old rattlesnake flag, 'Don't Tread On Me.' If, before November, you publish any allegations attacking me and the

Bay Psalm Book, I will sue you for libel, and believe me, I will win and strip you down to your last red cent. You would be calling me a liar and a crook, and as for monetary damage, you would be forcing me to defend against an IRS investigation of my claim for a tax deduction, and if the polls showed even a few percentage points of a drop in my popular support and voluntary campaign contributions—well, do you get the message?"

"Loud and clear. I assure you there will be no *unsubstantiated* allegations."

"Good. To be blunt, speaking for the moment as your legal counsel, you would be well advised to keep your mouth shut."

He offered a valedictory handshake, which Cliff accepted with the respect of one gladiator for another. "And now I must be off to a luncheon engagement. By all means keep me posted on anything you find out about Schofield."

Winthrop clapped Cliff on the shoulder and gave him his finest smile. "And keep wearing that pin! Looks good on you! We may yet become the best of friends!"

They parted and Cliff left, figuratively covered with so peculiar an emulsion of soft soap and blood that even Mrs. Roscommon raised her eyebrows.

Goldina Fuller broke into a delighted smile when she opened her door. "Why, Dr. Dunbar! You haven't forgotten me!"

"Now, how could I do that?"

"I suppose you couldn't, if you have fallen victim to my charms."

"To be truthful, it was your iced tea as much as it was your charms."

"My! You don't wear your heart on your sleeve, do you? Well, all right, come in and have a glass. You're worse than Abe."

When she returned from the kitchen, again bearing a pitcher of her love potion, she said, "How is your investigation going?"

"Things are getting very interesting." He filled her in on Mona's proofreading, the attack in the parking lot, and his visit with Winthrop. She listened closely, occasionally exclaiming, "Gracious! For pity's sake!"—and, upon hearing Winthrop's warning that he keep his mouth shut, "If that doesn't take the rag off the bush!"

"Which brings me to the reason for my visit. Did you really mean it when you said I could call on you for help?"

"Of course. What can I do for you?"

"This may be too much to ask. If it is, say so. But I'd like you to volunteer your services at Winthrop's headquarters."

"Bluh."

"I gather you don't like him."

"He's a flimflam man if I ever saw one. A whited sepulcher."

"I agree, but luckily you don't have to like him."

"What do you want me to do over there?"

"I don't know exactly. I suppose I'd like to know who his visitors are—any unusual ones, anyway. And who his vendors are: people he does business with, who makes his plastic brooms, who does his printing, and so on. General information."

"That shouldn't be difficult."

"But look out for Mrs. Roscommon. She's both suspicious and shrewd."

"I'll go over there Monday morning."

"I'd also like to invite you over to my house with a few other people, Sunday a week from tomorrow, at noon, say. For lunch and perhaps a swim in the pool."

"I'll be delighted to come for lunch and conversation. However, I burned my last bathing suit twenty years ago."

Cliff frowned. "I'm sorry, Mrs. Fuller, but I don't allow skinny-dipping."

"Oh, *you*! If we're getting that informal, I think you'd better start calling me Goldina."

"And you can call me Cliff."

"Let's hold it to Clifford for the time being."

"Clifford it is," he said, grinning.

"I hope you do find out who killed poor Mr. Schofield. I miss him all the more now, because a young man who's taking piano lessons has moved into his old apartment."

"A beginner?"

"He spends a full hour every afternoon trying to get through 'Do Ye Ken John Peel' without a mistake. It's so provoking. He stops at that high note just before the run at the second 'break of day,' and I can just *see* him getting his fingers arranged in the right bunches."

"Working for Winthrop will have its advantages, then."

"One, at least."

Akira couldn't believe what he heard Cliff saying over the phone. "You've got to be kidding, Cliff."

"I know it's a hell of a thing to ask, but things are heating up, and time is getting to be a consideration."

"The answer is still no. I can't let you take the *Bay Psalm Book* home with you, for God's sake! You must think I'm crazy. I know you are."

"We could risk it just for the weekend, couldn't we? I've got a wall safe in my house, and I'm having bars put over the windows today."

"No, we couldn't. I don't even want to *think* about what they'd do to me if that book got lost or damaged. I'd have to go back to slinging lugs of lettuce and tomatoes for my old man. And how about you? What if you got knifed like Link? *Iie, anjin-san!*"

"Okay! *Watakushi-wa,* Akira-*san!*"

"Tell you what I'll do, though. I'll photocopy it for you. You don't have to have the original at home just for proofreading."

"That'd be swell, Akira, but I hate to make you spend Saturday afternoon copying a book."

"Listen, I'm so glad I wasn't sucker enough to let you take it home that it'll be a pleasure. I'll leave my apartment now and meet you at the library in half an hour."

*   *   *

Mona met him at the door when he arrived home late in the afternoon carrying a bundle of copied sheets.

"Those guys were *fast!*" she said. "They've already installed bars over all the windows in the house except for that small one in the utility room and the odd-shaped ones in the two bathrooms. Also, they didn't know whether you'd want to bother with quick-release mechanisms for those small windows."

"No, I don't think so."

"Also, the man from that other shop put in the two peepholes you wanted in the front door and the wall, and he's got the wrought-iron gate all wired and everything, but he needs a special spring and hinge for closing it that he didn't have with him. He says he'll put it on tomorrow if he's got one in the shop, and Monday morning if he doesn't."

"Terrific. I'm glad you were here to handle all this. I've had a busy day."

"You can tell me all about it over dinner. We're having baked ham and pineapple, candied yams, asparagus, and a bottle of Buena Vista chardonnay. You live well, Monsieur le Professeur."

"Evidently you cook well, Mademoiselle Moore."

"You bet your life. I have to eat here, too."

They dined by candlelight, with pink camellias floating in a cut-crystal bowl.

Mona raised her glass. "Well, here's to the world of proofreading! Romantic, isn't it?"

"To the gunwales. Is my virtue in danger?"

"Not till the semester is officially over," said Mona.

"You're protecting me?"

"Right. We don't want any headlines reading, 'Professor-Student Love Nest Exposed.'"

"No use. Your being here is already incriminating. And staying all night."

"I'll deny everything. All I did was some proofreading."

"A likely story."

"Your alumni bulletin came today. There's an article about you in it."

"The Chaucer story?"

"Yes. I was impressed. You've become sort of famous."

"Within a very-small-diameter circle, yes. Chaucer wrote two versions of the Prologue to *The Legend of Good Women*, and scholars have argued for a hundred years over which came first, the A version or the B version. I nailed it down conclusively that it has to be the B version."

"How did you do it?"

"Mostly internal reference, starting with the God of Love telling Chaucer to give the poem to the queen at Eltham or at Shene."

"Uh-huh."

"Eltham and Shene were castles that were destroyed in 1394, the year of Queen Anne's death, and—uh—so now I'm famous. However, I don't think you'll impress the guys down at the gas station telling them you know me. Tell 'em I'm a blackjack expert instead, and I usually win money when I go to Vegas."

"Is that true?"

"Sure. To kill time between Viet Cong ambushes, Sergeant Fixico taught me his card-counting system. It works. Do you realize your hair is exactly the same color as the wine?"

"Of course. That's why I didn't serve rosé. And in exchange for the compliment, tell you what: I'll play a few songs for you after dinner. That's a fine guitar you have. I played it this afternoon."

"Swell, but don't ask *me* to play anything. I know a C chord and a G chord and I fake the rest."

"I'll teach you the D7 and then you can play 'em all."

After dinner, still by candlelight, she took up the guitar and sang, with pure and moving simplicity, that most beautiful of American folk songs, "Oh, Shenandoah." And Cliff saw that she was truly beautiful.

"Mona, that was marvelous. It really touched me."

"I also know one medieval song I'll sing in your honor. It's Spanish." And she moved into the haunting minor chords and vibrato notes of the "Song of the Three Moorish Girls":

> *Tres móricas me enamoran en Xaén,*
> *Axa y Fatima y Marién . . .*

"And that's it for tonight, folks. Proofreading tomorrow." She put the guitar aside and stood up.

Cliff took her gently by the shoulders and said, "Good night, Mona, and thank you. That was a lovely treat."

She put her hands behind his shoulders, and their lips met, long enough to convey more than casual friendship, but parting well this side of passion, leaving glimmers of possibilities.

"Good night, Cliff," she said softly, and left him with an appraising smile.

TWELVE

*T*hey worked again on Sunday morning after eggs Benedict by the pool, which had now warmed to eighty-four degrees.

While Mona forged ahead with her proofreading, Cliff tried to telephone C. T. Post at Yale. The English Department secretary there informed him that Post had gone on a hiking trip on the Appalachian Trail and wouldn't be back for a week.

Cliff had no telephone number for Bradford Silliman at Oxford, so he composed a cable to send to him in care of the head librarian at the Bodleian. Inasmuch as he was asking a favor, he decided not to stint on words.

"My dear Silliman: When and if convenient, would you please check Bodleian copy of *Bay Psalm Book* for the following: Second page of Preface, second line from bottom, Winthrop copy has 'scriptures' not 'sciptures.' Psalm 23, first line, Winthrop copy has 'shepherd' not 'shepheard.' Would appreciate your calling me collect or cable to tell me what inferences you would draw from these discrepancies." He added his telephone number.

He had a struggle getting the woman at Western Union to take down the misspelled words exactly as he misspelled them. It stuck in her craw. She was a stickler for accuracy. She also insisted that the proper spelling for the library was probably "Bodleyan," citing "Wesleyan" as an analogy. Cliff reluctantly told her he was an English professor who had been there and should know. She accepted that grudgingly and read the message back to him, making one more try when she hit "inferences." Didn't Cliff mean "implications"? When he said absolutely not, she turned frosty in defeat.

"One last thing," said Cliff. "Please make sure you don't spell Silliman with a 'y' or my ass will be in a sling."

"You're no English professor!" she sniffed, snatching at a rag end of victory. "English professors don't talk like that."

"Got me! I'm actually a backhoe operator."

When he hung up, the phone rang instantly. It was Jack Lloyd, the man who was putting in the electrically controlled gate, phoning to say he would install the hinge and spring on Monday. Then the grillwork people called to verify that he was at home and they could finish their work with the window bars.

At noon he made tuna fish sandwiches and a pitcherful of iced tea, carefully following Goldina Fuller's instructions.

He and Mona swam in the pool and lunched under the umbrella. The presence of Mona in a sea-green bathing suit made it difficult for the two workers installing the grills to concentrate. Cliff was amused.

"You're costing me money, Mona. I'm paying those guys time and a half and you've got them mesmerized."

"I told you wait till you see me in a bathing suit."

"Yes, you did. And you do have . . . quite a nice figure."

"Ha! Caught you being the polite gentleman again! You thought I was under the delusion that I look like Tani of the South Seas. All I meant was I'm a healthy American girl without a scrap of fat on her."

In lieu of blushing, Cliff rubbed his bullet scar. "Damn it, stop reading my mind. And if you want to know the truth, sex goddesses bore me stiff."

"I knew that, too," she tittered. "Ouch!" she slapped her leg. "Mosquito."

"Big one?"

"About a size eighteen."

This time it was Cliff who was mesmerized. He stared at her. "Did you say, 'size eighteen'?"

"Yes. Maybe I should explain."

"You don't need to. My God, Mona, is it possible that you're a fly fisherman?"

"Sure, I've been one all my life. My dad taught me early. He and another teacher at Madras High run fly-fishing float trips down the Deschutes River in the summer. He should be on one right now. The salmon flies are hatching."

"Is there no end to your charms?"

"You're a fly fisherman, too?"

"Yes! Yes, I am!"

"I *thought* you were kind of crazy."

"Of course! You have to be, to be willing to stand in the middle of a river with your waders full of ice-cold water, to catch trout that cost you a hundred dollars a pound."

"Well, I'll be jiggered. You have a nice assortment of charms yourself. I think my father would like you. Well, back to the proofing again." She collected their dishes and headed for the house. The workmen sorrowfully returned to serious business.

At the kitchen door, she paused and looked back. "You're not so bad in a bathing suit yourself!"

Monday was a busy day. Jack Lloyd came and installed the hinge and spring on the wrought-iron gate. Together with the window bars, it turned the house into a veritable fortress. Goldina Fuller called to let him know they had welcomed her as a volunteer. Fred Collins, Winthrop's finance chairman and chief fund-raiser, called and asked if he might drop by that afternoon, say, two o'clock. Mona proofread through Psalm 80. Shortly before noon the phone rang and the operator asked if Cliff would accept a collect call from Oxford.

"Dr. Dunbar? Bradford Silliman here. How are you?"

"Fine. And you, sir?"

"Both good and bad, in the vein of those jokes the students are so fond of these days. The good part is that I just enjoyed the finest dinner I've ever had in England. The bad part—

strictly for me, I hardly need say, not for you—the bad part is that you are obviously onto something extremely odd about the *Bay Psalm Book*."

"You've already looked at it?"

"Today at the Bodleian. As I believe you know, the Bodleian's is the only perfect copy extant, besides Winthrop's. And the text of the Bodleian is identical with that of the Dodd, Mead facsimile—and, I'm sure, with all the other extant copies. Have you had Post examine the Yale copy?"

"No, he's off on a hiking trip for a week."

"Have him take a look when he gets back, but he's sure to find the same thing I did. Neither of the two spellings you asked about occurs in the Bodleian copy."

"What would you surmise from that?"

"One of two things. The Winthrop copy is either a separate printing in the same year of 1640, or else it's a forgery of unknown date—but I'm completely flummoxed. Do you realize it's a remote possibility that the Winthrop copy is actually the *first* printing and all the other copies are the *second*? If so, the Winthrop copy would be absolutely unique and even more valuable than the others. However, I consider that so unlikely as to be preposterous. Why on earth would Stephen Daye, the printer, take the trouble to alter a mere two words in either version, when both of them are shot with errors?"

"That's what my proofreader says, and I agree."

"That leaves the possibility of a forgery, but if it is one, it's a masterpiece. In the meantime, I would advise you to scrutinize it very closely indeed. Pay particular attention to the paper."

"I'll do that. And thank you very much, Dr. Silliman. I'm greatly indebted to you."

"Glad to do it. This has turned into a very interesting problem. And may I say that I am also indebted to you?"

"In what way?"

"You inspired me with your talk about Mount Silliman. You made me realize how flabby and overweight I've become.

Have you ever noticed how many English professors die in
their sixties? I have resolved to get myself back into shape.
I'm not jogging yet, but I've started off by walking a brisk five
miles every morning."

"That's marvelous, Dr. Silliman. I look forward to the hike
with you."

"Excellent. And I think we'd better put ourselves on a first-
name basis. Please call me Brad."

"And I'm Cliff."

"Good luck with the book, Cliff."

Goldina Fuller phoned him from a restaurant at twelve-
fifteen. "Clifford? It's Goldina. I'm on my lunch break, and I
need it! It's been a hectic morning."

"What are they having you do?"

"Mostly orientation so far. They had me study Perry Winthrop's platform and a sort of manifesto of his principles,
which sounds more like an instruction book on how to demol-
ish a building, and tomorrow they plan to set me to canvass-
ing small-business executives, since I'm the widow of one.
Abe was in bag and twine, you know."

"Did they introduce you to Winthrop?"

"No, and I'm glad. I would never vote for that man. I think
he's a scalawag, and he's surrounded by scalawags. That
lawyer Fred Collins spent an hour with him this morning,
and they both came out looking like sharks on the prowl for a
swimmer."

"I think I'm the swimmer. Collins is coming to see me this
afternoon."

"Don't let him get near your legs. Now, then—do you have a
pencil? I have collected a good deal of information. Winthrop
spent a half hour this morning with the head of a local retail
clerks' union, Walter Paxson, who came out gnashing his
cigar, and an hour with the head of the Citizens for Winthrop
organization, Dr. Leon Gates, who came out looking like Boss
Tweed. The plastic brooms are manufactured by the New Era
Novelty Company, 2140 Pacific Boulevard, Los Angeles.

That's close to Abe's factory. The campaign posters and literature are printed by Loren Brewner Press, 806 Division Street,
South Pasadena. That's spelled B-r-e-w-n-e-r."

"Nice work, Goldina."

"That Mrs. Roscommon informed me that Brewner Press
does printing and binding for the famous Huntington Library
in San Marino and furnishes the campaign literature at
below cost."

"I've heard of Brewner Press, but I'm surprised they bother
with this kind of work."

"I hope all this has helped you."

"Only time will tell."

"How long do you want me to stay on there?"

"Can you manage two or three more days?"

"I suppose—if only to get a rest from 'John Peel.' Well, I'd
better stir my stumps. I'm having lunch with two old chick-
abiddies I work with. They're nice enough, but they haven't
got a lick of sense. They think Perry Winthrop simply came
down from heaven in a golden chariot."

The imminent visit from Fred Collins reminded Cliff that he
had heard the name somewhere before, and in a context
unconnected with politics. The notion puzzled him. As he
thought about it, he became aware that he was visualizing
sheets of white paper with blue stripes on it. Computer
printouts, of course.

He rummaged among the papers on his desk and extracted
the printouts that Shirley Mow had given him in the library.
He found only repeated references to Collins as Perry Winthrop's confidant and fund-raiser. Oh, well. He stacked the
sheets neatly again, glancing idly at the top one, one of the
printouts on Floretta Bishop. The citation list at the end
caught his eye.

"NAME DATA: BISHOP, FLORETTA. LAPIDUS, MEYER
'SOCKS.' LAPHAM, ROGER. COLLINS, G. FREDERICK."

He glanced at the news abstracts: "RELEASED ON HA-
BEAS CORPUS SUBMITTED BY HER ATTORNEY, G.

FREDERICK COLLINS" ... "DEFENSE ATTY. G. FRED-
ERICK COLLINS, MS. BISHOP'S COUSIN ..."

Cousin? Of course, there must be a host of Fred Collinses in
the world, but he pondered the links of association that
sprang to mind: Collins, Bishop, Winthrop, Las Vegas.

At one-fifteen he called Phil Fixico, not expecting to get him
at that hour, but he did.

"Jungle Jim! What's happenin'?"

"How come you're there, Phil? I thought Hollywood agents
took three-hour lunches."

"Not this rose, man. I'm not that big-time yet. What can I
do for you?"

"This is a wild, far-out hunch, Phil, but have you ever
booked any of your clients into the Mirage Hotel in Vegas?"

"The Ali Baba Room? Sure, three or four of them over the
past few years. Some of them repeats."

"Were contracts signed?"

"You better believe it."

"Can you tell me who signed for Mirage?"

"I could look it up. You want to hang on, or shall I call you
back?"

"I don't know. If you could check two or three contracts."

"In that case, hang on."

He hung on, listening to the background noise of tele-
phones, music, and a TV program in Phil's office. Add one
more profession Cliff was glad not to be in.

"Here we are," said Phil. "I found four with no sweat, and
all four are signed by one G. Frederick Collins, attorney for
Mirage Enterprises, Inc."

"Jesus Christ."

"I gather a bell has rung?"

"Big Ben, plus the Nine Tailors. Thanks a million."

"You *will* explain all this to me sometime, I hope."

"How about lunch and a swim here on Sunday around
noon?"

"You're on. See you then."

* * *

Fred Collins came through the wrought-iron gate at Cliff's front door promptly at two and rang the bell. Cliff saw through the peephole that he was carrying an attaché case— why, Cliff couldn't fathom, since they had initiated no paperwork. He surmised that the case was a mere prop, to impress him.

Cliff ushered him into the library, sizing him up on the way. Collins certainly didn't look like the stereotype of a Vegas lawyer—no shiny black alligator shoes, no silk shirts, no Krugerrand on a golden chain. He was dressed more like those accountants from Price Waterhouse who pad up to the rostrum on Academy Awards night and hand envelopes to Charlton Heston and Shirley MacLaine. He wore ordinary black oxfords, gray suit, white shirt, navy tie with gray stripes, black onyx cufflinks. He was one of those almost-too-handsome men with platinum hair and black eyebrows. He moved with total poise, confident that every time the envelope is opened, the MC will announce, "And the winner is . . . G. Frederick Collins."

"Well, Mr. Collins, what can I do for you?"

"We'll see. Perhaps we can do something for each other. I advised Perry Winthrop this morning that it would be wise for me to come have a talk with you. He consented, and here I am."

"Could I offer you a drink? It's a hot day."

"No, thanks."

"I make sensational iced tea."

Williams was derailed momentarily. "Iced tea? No—nothing, thanks."

"Ah. Well, proceed, counsel."

Collins sized up Cliff further for a moment, seemed to make some mental revision, and proceeded.

"You called on Perry Winthrop the other day to talk about Lincoln Schofield and the *Bay Psalm Book*, correct?"

"Correct."

"And Perry got upset and said several things to you—even

made threats—that I regard as injudicious, to say the least. He shouldn't have lost his temper in the first place, and that business about instituting a libel suit in the middle of his campaign sounds a little crazy—even if he could win it, which as a lawyer I doubt."

"Winthrop's a lawyer."

"Yes, and he's also a politician under terrific strain. He yielded to his emotions instead of using rational judgment, and I have warned him to guard against that. One small lapse and the public will turn thumbs down on a candidate, no matter how good he is. Look at what happened to Romney and Muskie, for example."

"Look, if you came here to apologize for him, there's no need to. I understand perfectly."

"I'm not apologizing, I'm explaining—partly to assure you that you need have no fear of libel suits."

"I wasn't really worried."

"Good. But to get to my object in coming here: I'm aware that you've been scrutinizing the *Bay Psalm Book* and that you have serious reservations about it."

"Right."

"May I ask you what grounds you have?"

"Sure. Certain inconsistencies between it and the other known copies."

"You realize that if the book is some sort of facsimile reprint, it would have to have been printed at least fifty years ago because Perry remembers it in the family library when he was a little boy."

"If he's telling the truth."

"I assure you he is. And if family tradition has any weight, then the book, even if it is a facsimile, has to be at least a hundred years old or more."

"That's stretching it a little. If it were that old it certainly wouldn't be a facsimile. Nobody would bother. It would be a reprint or another edition."

"There you have it, then. At worst, it's still the *Bay Psalm Book*, am I right?"

"If it's that old, yes. If it isn't, no."

"But you don't know."

"Not yet."

"All right. In spite of the uncertainty, we want to make you a very generous offer."

"One I can't refuse?"

Collins gave him an icy smile. "No, one you'd be foolish to refuse. We're not particularly worried about the authenticity of the book, but we are worried about any kind of adverse publicity erupting in the middle of this campaign. You can understand that."

"After what the country has been going through these past few years, I certainly can."

"Exactly. Consequently, even though you haven't discovered anything to impugn the book's authenticity, your case—if I can call it that—has considerable nuisance value to us. So we're prepared to offer you twenty-five thousand dollars if you'll merely call off your research for the time being."

"No."

"We're not asking you to drop it permanently. Just till after the election."

"I'm sorry, but no."

"Do you want to make a counteroffer?"

"No."

Collins heaved a sigh of a much-put-upon defense attorney confronted with a plaintiff who wants the moon and won't accept a reasonable settlement.

"Very well, then, we're prepared to go as high as fifty thousand, but for that large a sum we'd ask you to drop the matter entirely."

"No deal. Not for any sum."

"You mean you wouldn't even drop it for a quarter of a million?"

"That's right. It's not that I have such lofty morals. If I were a poor man, I admit I'd be tempted. Luckily for me and my soul, I'm well off."

"Let's compromise: fifty thousand, and you can do anything you want after the election."

"Out of the question."

Collins registered amazed disgust. "Do you really dislike Perry Winthrop that much? You'd give up that much to see him defeated?"

"Hell no, Collins! I don't give a damn about Winthrop! If the people want him as governor, swell. As far as I'm concerned, they can throw an ermine cape across his shoulders and anoint him the High and Mighty Duke de Kakiak of Baldwin Park!"

"Then what do you want?"

"Two things: the killer or killers of Lincoln Schofield, and scholarly honesty."

"And you still think the book has something to do with his murder."

"I think it very likely."

Collins stood up and turned away from Cliff, sunk in thought, one hand on his hip, the other rubbing the back of his neck.

"Dr. Dunbar," he said, turning to him again, "I don't think you realize what you're up against. I want to choose my words very carefully now, because I don't want you to misconstrue my meaning as anything resembling a threat. Forgive me if I misspeak myself anyway. You've been an English professor for some time, and that's a rather cloistered world where ideals can flourish—mainly because they're safely remote from the rough-and-tumble realities of the political world, which is marked by pragmatism, compromise, approximations to ideals, and, occasionally, brass knuckles."

"It may surprise you to hear that English departments are like that, too."

"Perhaps. But it's a matter of scale. Departmental squabbles are just that: squabbles over trivia among a handful of people. But have you any conception of the enormous stakes involved in a major election—and of the enormous forces pitted against each other? This isn't a contest to see who gets academic tenure. We're talking about the governorship of California, perhaps followed by a Senate seat, and even a shot at the presidency."

"So what's your point?"

"That many powerful individuals and powerful groups have a huge stake in this election—so huge that some of them willingly and ruthlessly would crush anyone who stands in their way. Conceivably, some of them might even consider violence. I can't imagine who, but it's possible. Or they might adopt more devious means."

"Such as what?"

"Such as finding something wrong with the title deed to your house, or having your house seized under eminent domain for the construction of a power station or a park, or having the IRS conduct an endless investigation of your tax returns, or raking up embarrassing secrets, such as your forfeiture of pay and allowances for disobeying a direct order to lead an attack in Vietnam."

"So you've already done some raking."

"Of course I have. I'm in politics and I have a great deal at stake."

"Okay, thanks for the warning. I'll be careful."

"Do that. And think over our offer. Call me if you change your mind, as I'm sure you will, because you strike me as a rational man."

"You're wrong, Mr. Collins. I'm one of the crazies. I won't be calling."

"I think you will. We'll see."

He retrieved his attaché case, and Cliff saw him out.

From the living-room window, Mona watched him back his black Mercedes onto Sunset Boulevard. Cliff came and stood beside her.

"I listened through the library door," she said. "Hope you don't mind. That man scares me. Did he scare you?"

"Yep."

"In spite of all that business about misspeaking and misconstruing, it sounded like a real threat to me. Did it to you?"

"Beyond a doubt."

"Who do you suppose those unknown violent people are?"

"Could be anybody. Political fanatics. Loyal henchmen. A lone kook. But you know what really gives me the fantods? This finger that keeps pointing toward Las Vegas. I don't even like to think about what's implied by the linkup of Fred Collins, cousin Floretta, Socks Lapidus, the Mirage Casino, Italo Pellegrino—and Perry Winthrop."

"The Mafia?"

"If I'm not being melodramatic."

"Know what I think? I think it's time for you to turn the whole thing over to Lieutenant Puterbaugh, and let's go fishing. In Oregon."

"I'd hate to do that. What do we turn over to him? A pair of typographical errors?"

"Not exactly an oriental dagger of curious design, is it?"

"Hardly. But if push comes to shove and it really *is* the Mafia—well, call me chicken, but I'll run to Lieutenant Puterbaugh as fast as my chubby little legs will take me. I have no desire to play the leading role in *One Man Against the Mafia*."

"I don't want you to, either."

"But what would I tell Pearl?"

"The truth; she'd understand. But what do you think we should do right now?"

"Finish the proofing. How's it going?"

"I'm almost finished. And I haven't found a darn thing more except a funny-looking smudge on a page numbered Gg3."

"A smudge?"

"The bottom of a word is smeared slightly. Come take a look."

She showed him the photocopied page.

"Peculiar," he said. "Could have been the copier, though, I suppose."

"Could be; but I'd like to see what the original is like."

"We'll check it at the library tomorrow."

"Why not now?"

"Because I'm running out to the Huntington Library to see Larry Archer—one of the librarians."

"Can I go, too?"

"Better not. Things seem to be coming to a head, and I want you safe. Stay here, finish your proofing, lock the doors, and keep my pistol handy."

THIRTEEN

*F*rom a file drawer he took several sheets of lecture notes he used in teaching the second semester of Survey of English Literature and tucked them into his attaché case. Just like Fred Collins, he thought wryly.

San Marino, near Pasadena, is a suburb composed of million-dollar houses surrounded by green trees, lush flower beds, and emerald-green lawns urged on once a month by Gro-Rite and edging on curving, immaculately clean streets. But the place could almost be considered Skid Row in comparison with the mansion and former residence of Collis P. Huntington, the railroad magnate, now the Huntington Library.

The mansion stands in an extensive park, wooded here and there, with curving footpaths through the greenery. It is so beautiful that, bent on his mission as he was, Cliff couldn't resist treating himself to a visit to the Japanese house and garden tucked away in a grove of trees, especially to see once more the superb array of bonsai, and, among the bonsai, especially the grove of tiny maples standing in their tray on a mossy slope, through which gleamed a few miniature white boulders.

Then he entered the main building and paid a brief visit to Sir Thomas Lawrence's "Pinky," her fresh English flesh tones, and her gauzy dress moving slightly in the breeze.

He walked down the dark and gleaming hardwood floor of a high-ceilinged hall and entered Larry Archer's office.

Archer was hunched over his desk meticulously copying, onto three-by-five cards, an entry from the *General Catalogue of the British Museum.* He looked up with pleasure when Cliff walked in, and he rose to shake his hand.

"Clifford! How are you?"

"Fine—to give you a time-saving answer."

"But otherwise incredibly ensnarled?"

"That's about it. Am I interrupting you?"

"No, no. Merely jotting down data on a couple of items Rouse touted us onto. I'm hoping to arrange a trade with the British Museum, but if all else fails, we'll try money."

"Handy stuff, isn't it? Nice that Huntington knew how to rake it in."

"Indeed it is. It's not a popular sentiment these days, but have you ever considered the enormous debt scholars owe to the old magnates—Morgan, Carnegie, Folger, Huntington? Who else could have amassed the great collections? And I think the Huntington is the greatest."

That was apparent. Pride in being a Huntington librarian glowed from Archer. He resembled a pirate more than he did a curator of rare books, however. He stood six feet, four inches tall, broad-shouldered, muscular, with a wicked black moustache in a rough face deeply pitted from either smallpox or acne. He was a karate expert and a fine sailor, to boot.

"Getting in a lot of sailing this year?" Cliff asked.

"No, I'm selling my boat."

"You're kidding! *Old Fibersides?* How can you part with her?"

"I'm tired of racing, and the slip fees and upkeep are killing me. I'll rent a Hobie Cat when I feel the urge. I hear you're making a change yourself."

"That's right. I'll be at liberty at the end of the month."

"It'll be a loss to scholarship. Your Chaucer article was a magnificent piece of detection."

"Thanks partly to your help."

"And I thank you for the acknowledgment in the footnote."

"I won't be any great loss to the teaching profession, though, Larry. I really should have been a librarian, like you.

My great love isn't so much the classroom as it is books."

"No openings here at the moment," Archer said, grinning. "But we'll be happy to keep your application on file. Is there anything else I can do for you?"

"Yes. You can tell me if the Brewner Press does work for you."

"Oh, sure. They do quality printing and binding for us. They're the best in Southern California."

"Is that a business name, or is there a real Loren Brewner?"

Archer burst out laughing. "I'll say there is! And he's a genuine, blown-in-the-glass original, let me tell you! You don't know about Brewner?"

Cliff shook his head.

"One of the most remarkable characters you could ever hope to meet. He was a cowboy—a real cowboy—when he was young in Wyoming or Colorado, and a bronco threw him into a corral fence and shattered both his legs. They never did knit right, so he got a job as a printer's apprentice in town. And that was the origin of Brewner Press."

"A cowboy printer?"

"And he's never forgotten it. He has a gun collection you wouldn't believe, and he still looks like a cowboy. He wears western shirts with snaps on the pockets, he rolls his own, and his lingo is straight out of the bunkhouse. But don't let him fool you. Underneath all the rawhide is a highly intelligent mind. Once he couldn't ride anymore, he started to read—every book he could get his hands on, including technical books on printing. He's an authority on the American West, but I wouldn't be surprised if he could pass an exam in your Survey of English Lit right now. You ought to go see him. He's one of a kind."

"I was planning to."

"But Jesus, Cliff, try not to rub him the wrong way. He's a gallant gentleman when it comes to what he calls 'the ladies,' but he can take an instant dislike to men, and if he does, he won't take your business or have anything to do with you."

"Whom does he dislike?"

"Oh, anybody he thinks looks like a hippie, gays, Socialists, rock musicians—and worst of all, people who know very little about books and printing but try to fake it."

"How do *you* get along with him?"

"Fine, as long as we stay off politics and Pink Floyd. Mind you, I've had my ups and downs with him, but stap my vitals if he doesn't do magnificent work! He also has a great collection of historic type fonts. We even use them from time to time."

"Type fonts?"

"Yes, enough to start a respectable museum of typography."

"You wouldn't know if he owns Stephen Daye's font?"

"The man who printed the *Bay Psalm Book*? I don't think he could. That font was given to Harvard way back when. I believe that was the start of Harvard University Press. I'm sure he has some seventeenth- and eighteenth-century fonts, though. Why?"

"It's possible—barely possible—that he may have used one to forge something."

"Jesus, I hope not! I don't want the old curmudgeon in the clink! We need him."

"We'll see. I may be wrong. I think I'll run over and see him now."

"Better hurry. He closes at five, and when that door shuts he wouldn't open it for Johann Gutenberg."

South Pasadena is only minutes from San Marino. Cliff arrived in front of Brewner Press on Division Street at four-forty. A passerby would scarcely notice the place, sandwiched in among expensive antique shops. It had no large identifying signs, merely small gilt letters on the show window reading, "Brewner Press—Fine Printing and Binding." Two open folio volumes from the eighteenth century stood propped on easels in the window; between them lay a volume of *Edgar A. Poe's Poetical Works* newly bound in full green morocco with gilt edges. Not so much as a card boasted that Brewner had done the binding.

Before he walked in, Cliff briefly considered what role he would play. If Brewner recognized him, of course, the jig was up. Otherwise, he resolved to rub Brewner the wrong way and see what came of it. He opened the door and entered the shop.

No one was behind the counter. The place was spotless and, unlike any printing shop Cliff had ever seen, uncluttered with papers and vendors' calendars. The only wall decorations consisted of a Winthrop campaign poster ("Vote for Winthrop—the New Broom") and a series of blown-up samples of typefaces behind nonreflecting glass: Century Book, Caslon, Garamond, Baskerville, the italics designed by Aldus Manutius of Venice, William Morris's type design for the Kelmscott Chaucer. One sample in particular captured his attention. It was the charming obituary that Benjamin Franklin composed for himself:

> The body of
> Benjamin Franklin, printer
> (Like the cover of an old book,
> Its contents worn out,
> And stript of its lettering and gilding)
> Lies here, food for worms!
> Yet the work itself shall not be lost,
> For it will, as he believed, appear once more
> In a new
> And more beautiful edition,
> Corrected and amended
> By its Author!

But the interesting feature was the typeface—clearly old, with its kerned "j" in "Benjamin" and several kerned "f's" that looked like "s's" in the old style. Very much like Stephen Daye's font. Cliff studied it intently.

"Well, what do *you* want?" said a gruff voice behind him.

"Oh! I was looking for Mr. Brewner."

"You're looking at him. I ain't screwed to the wall."

"Oh! Well! Yes, of course!"

The man behind the counter scowled at him through thick bifocals that made his eyes look huge and predatory as an owl's. He was about sixty-two or sixty-three, tall, thinning iron-gray hair, head thrust forward from a yellow-and-white-checked flannel shirt and a bolo tie clipped together with a silver and turquoise kachina.

"My name is Kerry Arbogast, Mr. Brewner. I saw your ad in the Yellow Pages."

Brewner let this piece of news whiz by him low and outside. He continued to stare at Cliff.

"I have something I'd like printed. The ad says you do fine printing."

"I'm the best in this man's town. What've you got?"

"Well, I'm something of a poet, don't you know, and I've written a sonnet cycle—a hundred sonnets, to be exact. And I'd like to have, oh, say two hundred copies printed on good rag bond paper to present it to, you know, family and friends?"

"Got a sample?"

"What do you need one for? All sonnets are fourteen lines."

"I want to know whether I'll print it or not."

"You mean—if you don't like something, you won't print it?"

"That is correct."

"Rather a novel viewpoint for a printer, isn't it? I thought the customer was always supposed to be right."

"In my experience, half the people who come through that door are assholes."

"Oh! Well! I suppose you do run into some odd types, dealing with the general public."

"Do you have a sample or not?"

"Why, yes, if you insist." Cliff fumbled in his briefcase and extracted a typewritten sheet.

Brewner glanced at it and said, "Miltonic."

"Yes. But the cycle is a mixture of that plus Petrarchan and Shakespearean."

Brewner gave him a glance containing a glimmer of approval and read the sonnet.

> When winds that move not its calm surface sweep
> The azure sea, I love the land no more;
> The smiles of the serene and tranquil deep
> Tempt my unquiet mind.—But when the roar
> Of Ocean's gray abyss resounds, and foam
> Gathers upon the sea, and vast waves burst,
> I turn from the drear aspect to the home
> Of earth and its deep woods, where intersperst,
> When winds blow loud, pines make sweet melody.
> Whose house is some lone bark, whose toil the sea,
> Whose prey the wondering fish, an evil lot
> Has chosen.—But I my languid limbs will fling
> Beneath the plane, where the brook's murmuring
> Moves the calm spirit, but disturbs it not.

"Not bad," Brewner managed to concede.

Cliff thought so too, it being Shelley's translation from the Greek of a poem by Moschus.

"The ocean theme runs through quite a few of them. I'm something of a sailor, too, you see."

"Bullshit."

"I beg your pardon?"

"If you're a sailor, my ass is a soda fountain."

"Oh, I don't mean to imply I'm Barnacle Bill, exactly, just a day sailor, but I've won quite a few races."

"Where's the rest of 'em?"

"The rest of what? Oh—the sonnets? They're at home. You mean you'll print them?"

"I'll print 'em."

"Good. I'd like to have them on laid chain paper if that's possible. Maybe six-by-nine pages with gilt edges, like the Poe in the window?"

"I can handle that."

"And since they're sort of old-fashioned, I thought they'd look nice in one of the old typefaces, like Franklin's obituary there. Seventeenth- or eighteenth-century. Seventeenth, if you can do it."

"Do you know the difference between seventeenth- and eighteenth-century faces?"

"Well, actually, no, not really."

"Then why the hell specify one of 'em? Leave that to me."

"All right. Of course."

"But for your information—yes, I have seventeenth-century fonts. How do you want the books bound?"

"I was thinking of full morocco."

Brewner glared at him, breathing heavily in and out of his nostrils, his head bobbing up and down as if apoplexy were imminent.

"Is there something wrong with morocco?" Cliff asked.

"No, it's the best there is."

"Then let's use it."

"No."

"Don't you have any?"

"Yeah, I've got a stack of red morocco. Some green."

"Then what's the problem?"

"Let me tell you about morocco, mister. It's a rare commodity. It comes from goatskin. Over in Morocco, you know what the goatherd's main job is? All day long, it's to keep the goats from butting each other and spoiling the leather. After months of that, they skin the goat, peel off the top grain, tan it, dye it, and ship it. And I'll be a son-of-a-bitch if I'm going to waste it on some amateur's vanity press book of poems."

"I guess you save it for the Huntington."

"That is correct. And besides that, have you got any idea what it would cost you to hand-compose fourteen hundred lines of movable type and print and bind two hundred copies in full morocco?"

"No, I don't."

"We're talking about ten or fifteen thousand dollars."

"Ouch! However, I've got the money."

"Not for morocco, you don't. If you've got to have leather, you can go to half calf."

"Let's make it that, then. I'll bring in the whole manuscript in a day or two. . . . By the way, I gather from that poster on the wall that you're for Winthrop."

"Anybody who isn't is a goddamn fool."

"Another precinct heard from! Heh, heh, heh."

That earned Cliff another scowl.

"I'm not only for him, I do his printing free gratis."

"Must be effective. Looks as if he'll win."

"Yeah. Maybe this state isn't the political loony bin it used to be, electing two Browns, a Warren, and a Reagan. Now get the hell out of here. I'm locking up."

"May I take a couple of your brochures?"

"Help yourself."

"He's got to be the one, wouldn't you say?" asked Mona.

"He's a red-hot candidate."

"You don't think he recognized you?"

"Not unless he's the greatest deadpan actor since Buster Keaton, or he's blind as a bat. His glasses look like ice cubes. How about the proofing? Find anything more?"

"Not a thing. We still need that smoking pistol."

"I'm dubious about that now. I don't think my amazing powers of detection are going to turn up a smoking pistol. If one shows up, it'll have to be an act of God. I almost hope I'll get attacked again."

"Bite your tongue!"

"It'd be something to go on."

"Dear, I don't want to have to solve *your* murder. And besides, if they get you they might get me, and I don't want to go."

"But that sounds rather romantic—our going together, like Romeo and Juliet, Paolo and Francesca, Pyramus and Thisbe . . ."

"Huh-uh. I'll take Prince Charles and Diana any day. If I'm going to be attacked, I want it to be with Cupid's arrow."

"That reminds me. I want to call Archer."

He caught Archer as he was going out to dinner.

"I'll keep you only a second, Larry. This afternoon you said you and Brewner had had your ups and downs. What kind of ups and downs?"

"Oh, besides the usual clash of opinions, once in a great while I was unhappy with the work he did—very rarely, of course. But Brewner can get high-handed as hell. There was one printing job, for example—a monograph on our Jacobean collection—that he unilaterally decided to make a four-color job when I clearly told him we wanted only black and white. He thought black and white 'looked cheap' and went ahead with color—and insisted on being paid for it."

"So you bitched like hell and paid him."

"You got to know him very well this afternoon, didn't you?" They shared a laugh.

"The only real run-in we had was a little over a year ago, though. It was a rebinding job on a seventeenth-century encyclopedia of natural philosophy—which in those days meant all of the known sciences."

"I know."

"Of course. You would. Anyway, this set of books was falling apart. The spines were cracked, the calf covers were crumbling and falling apart, a few title pages needed mending—you name it. We sent the set to Brewner and he stripped off the old covers, took all the gatherings apart, restitched and reglued and rebound the whole set in new calf. Beautiful job. But you know how some old printers used to bind in several extra blank fly leaves front and back?"

"Sure. Do go on."

"Well, these volumes had eight extra fly leaves front and back—four folded folios—but they came back to us with only two. I called Brewner on it and he got very defensive and salty. Asked me what the hell I wanted—he had added beautiful marbled fly leaves on his own initiative. I told him we didn't want marbled fly leaves, he was missing the point—he had failed to preserve the original integrity of the set, and I wanted to know where the missing paper was. He said he'd check with his workmen, but he never did find it."

"How many volumes were in that set?"

"Twenty-four smallish folios."

"So if two blank folios were missing from each volume, somebody could print eight pages of text per volume, and eight times twenty-four is a hundred ninety-two possible pages."

Long pause at the other end.

"Larry?"

"I'm here. You're about to spoil my evening, aren't you?"

"I hope so."

"All right; what do you think he forged?"

"The *Bay Psalm Book*."

"Oh, my God."

"I can't absolutely prove it yet, but it looks likely."

"Lordy, how I hope you're wrong! Can you imagine the colossal stink this would raise?"

"Vividly."

"Winthrop . . . the election . . . and Brewner? They'll run them all out of the country!"

"Well, the people wanted a new broom."

FOURTEEN

Cliff drove to the LAU library with Mona the next morning. He found himself glancing frequently in his rear-view mirror, but no one seemed to be following them.

"I think someone will be, though. From here on out, Mona, we've both got to stay very much on the alert—unless, that is, I can drive you straight to the airport and fly you to Oregon, which I'd very much like to do."

"No."

"You've finished with your proofreading."

"I want to be here to see how this turns out. Besides, you owe me a pile of money."

"I'll write you a check."

"They wouldn't cash it in Oregon."

Akira Yonenaka was waiting for them. He beamed when they came in. "Ah, Mr. and Mrs. North! Welcome back to my miserable *bibliothèque!*"

"Thank you, Mr. Moto. May we examine the holy book once more?"

"Here on the table."

"What page was that, Mona?"

"Gg3."

They opened the book to page Gg3 and held it open with the two velvet bags.

"See?" said Mona. "The word 'juniper' *is* smudged at the bottom. It wasn't the copier."

Cliff touched the word with his index finger. "Peculiar. The paper seems sort of—stained."

"Stained?" said Akira. "Let me have a look at it."

He took up the book and examined it at a slant in the light from the western windows. "There's a patchy sheen in several spots on the page. It seems to be in some sort of pattern. See for yourselves."

They took turns examining the page from several angles but couldn't make anything out.

"Let me put it on the light box," said Akira. They followed him into his office. Akira pressed the switch on his light box. It flickered and came on. The pane of glass glowed with a cool blue-white illumination. He opened the book carefully and gently pressed page Gg3 flat on the glass.

As if printed in lemon juice, invisible letters sprang out from their hiding place under the text: upside down, on three lines, the letters or words "OR . . . ROP . . . ROOM."

"What do you suppose *that* is?" said Akira.

"Try page Gg2, Akira, and I think you'll find something amazing."

He flattened the page on the light box. More letters, these spelling "VOTE F . . . WINTH . . . THE NEW B."

Cliff banged his fist on the table. "Got him! That's it!"

"The smoking pistol!" exclaimed Mona.

"You bet your buttons!"

Cliff threw his arms around Mona and kissed her joyously.

"Shiver my timbers!" said Akira. "I see it, but what is it?"

"It's beautiful! Perfect! And there's no way Brewner or Winthrop can wriggle out of this one!"

"My Oriental shrewdness is failing me."

"Oh—you don't know about the paper." Cliff explained how Brewner had moonlighted old paper out of the encyclopedia.

"So here's what must have happened. Brewner had his type set up to print some small campaign placards, and the type had a light film of oil in it. And then he or somebody in his shop—but probably Brewner—carelessly laid a stack of that blank encyclopedia paper on it, and the oil offset the letters right onto the bottom sheet, which ended up on pages Gg2 and Gg3 in the book."

They consulted again.

"You mean," said Pudgy loudly, "if we strip down—maybe you won't call the cops?"

"That's right."

"You got a deal!"

Without their guns and without their uniforms, the tough guys turned into a pair of out-of-shape, middle-aged men with sagging bellies and bluish-white skin.

Cliff opened the door and waved them into the library with his pistol. Mona followed.

"Sit down, gentlemen."

They seated themselves stiffly on two leather chairs, facing Cliff behind his desk.

"That's a cute setup you got out there," said Pudgy sheepishly. "I gotta remember that one."

"You fellas from out of town?"

"Yeah. How'd you make us?" Gaunt inquired.

"Uniformed police in L.A. use black-and-whites. Only plainclothesmen travel in unmarked cars."

"Jeez!"

"Who're you working for?"

"Look, you aced us out, okay? Ain't that enough?"

"Not by a long chalk. I want to know who sent you."

"Man, we're probably dead already, you know that? And if we fink on our bosses, we really crap out. We'd be eighty-sixed in nothing flat."

"Sure. *Omertà* and all that."

"You got the picture."

"Okay. I give up. I'll call the cops instead."

"Hey! I thought you said if we stripped you wouldn't call the cops!"

"What the hell do you think I am, some kind of pervert? I don't get any kicks seeing you in your underwear, for chrissake!"

The eyebrows shot up on Gaunt's mournful face. "Did we even get the right house? You're a college professor?"

"Certainly."

"You sure as shit don't talk like one."

"You've been cutting too many classes."

"*Ha*!"

"Who's she?"

"A friend. Let's cut this short. I'll make a deal with you guys. You tell me who sent you, and I'll let you go."

"On the level? You mean just walk out of here?"

"That's right."

Gaunt looked at Pudgy. "What do you say we take a chance? We're gonna get iced one way or the other anyway."

"Not if nobody knows what happened here," said Cliff.

"I don't get you," said Pudgy.

"You give me the name, you walk out, and we forget the whole thing. You can say I was out of town, or you couldn't get at me, or any excuse you can think of."

"You really mean that? But you can snitch on us afterward."

"You'll just have to trust me. You don't have any other choice, do you? Let's go about it this way. You *don't* name any names. I do. For instance, do you know a man named Loren Brewner?"

"Never heard of him."

"How about Italo, or 'Tally,' Pellegrino?"

A very pregnant silence, in which Pudgy and Gaunt shifted uneasily in their chairs.

"Well, sure," said Pudgy. "Hell, everybody knows Tally."

"Is he the one who sent you?"

"Not exactly."

"Come on, is he or isn't he?"

"Man, you don't know what you're asking!"

"Does he know you?"

No answer.

"Would he be interested in knowing you're here? I'll be glad to phone him at the Mirage, and you can say hello." Cliff reached for the phone.

"Don't do that!" said Pudgy. "You win, Professor. I'll go as far as saying yes, it was associates of Tally who sent us, but that's as far as I go."

"That's good enough for me."

Gaunt and Pudgy relaxed somewhat.

"But I want it in writing."

"Oh, shit! You want us to fill out our own death warrant?"

"Don't worry. I don't intend to show it to anybody."

"What do you want it for, then?"

"Protection, mainly. Let's get to it."

Cliff gave them each a sheet of paper and a ballpoint pen. They wrote as he dictated a statement, starting with the date and attesting that they had attempted to murder Cliff at the instigation of associates of Italo Pellegrino. They signed themselves as Anthony Calcavecchia and Patrick Twomey. In his own mind, Cliff had dubbed them "Reedy" Pagliaccio and "Vesty" La Giubba. Not far off at that.

"Are those your real names?"

"Sure they are."

"Mona, run out and get their billfolds, will you? And lock up their weapons somewhere."

She hurried out.

"Cover all the bases, don't you?"

"Wouldn't you?"

Pudgy grinned. "Sure."

When Mona returned, Cliff looked at their driver's licenses. The pair were from Detroit, and the licenses bore the names they signed. Knowing the names could be aliases, however, Cliff had Mona take a Polaroid shot of Tony and Pat sitting near the desk in their underwear with their confessions visible.

"That's fine, Mona. Bring 'em their clothes now."

"It'll be a relief." She looked with professional disapproval at their unhealthy physiques and went out.

"Salty chick, ain't she?"

"She's a physical therapist."

When the two gunsels were dressed and ready to leave,

Pudgy turned to Cliff—who still held his pistol on them—and said, "Dunbar, you seem like a pretty regular guy. We got nothing personal against you, you know? This was strictly a business deal."

"Of course."

"So let me level with you. You haven't got a chance. We fumbled the job, but there'll still be a contract out on you. You know that."

"Not if I can get to Vegas fast enough."

"I hope you aren't taking those papers with you."

"I don't need to."

"Well, if you don't—thanks a million. We're taking an awful chance on you, but otherwise it's the slammer on one side and the mob on the other. Pat and I just can't take another stretch in the slammer. Not at our age."

"If I double-crossed you, you could always come back and take another crack at me."

"Yeah, I thought of that. So maybe we both got insurance."

"Certainly. If at first you don't succeed . . ."

"But no, thanks. I don't want to tangle with *you* again. You aren't the patsy they told us to expect."

Cliff unlocked the gate and ushered the two gunsels out. They strode briskly down the front sidewalk.

"*Ciao!*" Pudgy called out, waving without looking back.

Although neither Cliff nor Mona cared much for hard liquor, they agreed they deserved a good, stiff Wild Turkey old-fashioned. Cliff mixed them, complete with orange slice and maraschino cherry, while Mona swept up the debris in the entry hall.

They sank into chairs in the living room.

"You have me completely fooled, too," said Mona. "I thought that gate was to keep people out, not keep them in!"

"Oh, I'm slippery as a greased eel. . . . Got my wish, didn't I?"

"I hope you don't have three of them."

"I admire the way you kept your cool. That really helped."

"I'm pretty good in a crisis. The rubber knees come later. You're the one who's cool!"

"It was like Vietnam, only better. No jungle."

"What do you do now? You'd better do something fast if what that man said is true."

"About the contract on me? I'm hoping a phone call will fix that."

"Who to?"

"Tally Pellegrino."

"You think he'll call off the dogs?"

"If I can convince him Winthrop has had it, so that there's no point in killing me."

"What if you can't convince him?"

"Then I'm in real trouble. English teachers who buck the Mafia have a way of ending up lying in the desert out toward Pahrump, dotted with end punctuation. Do you know of a good hideout in Oregon?"

"Yes, a nice lake up near the Twin Sisters. If we go, bring the fixings for more old-fashioneds. This is terrific."

He finished his and headed for the phone in the library.

"Hey, can I have your cherry?" Mona said.

"Anytime," he replied without turning and ignored the ice cube that hit him in the back of the head.

He got the Mirage's phone number from Information.

"Mirage Hotel."

"Mr. Pellegrino, please."

"One moment."

"Mr. Pellegrino's office."

"May I speak to him, please?"

"May I ask who's calling?"

"Dr. Clifford Dunbar from Los Angeles."

"One moment."

After a long wait: "I'm sorry, but Mr. Pellegrino doesn't know you. Could you tell me the nature of your call?"

"Tell him I can prove Winthrop has blown the election."

"Winthrop has blown the election? One moment."

There was a loud click as someone picked up a receiver and a testy voice said, "What the hell is this?"

"Are you Tally Pellegrino?"

"Yeah, and who the hell are you?"

"Clifford Dunbar."

"I don't know any Clifford Dunbar."

"Tally, the book's a fake. The election is going to go blooey for Winthrop."

"Listen, mister, I don't know you and I don't know what kind of smoke you're trying to blow up my ass—so good-bye and don't call back!"

He hung up.

Cliff thumbed through the phone book.

"Now what?" said Mona.

"Mohammed will have to go to the mountain."

He was in luck. PSA had a cancellation on its early-afternoon flight to Las Vegas the next day. Cliff reserved the last two seats and promised to check in forty-five minutes before flight time.

"And we're off on the great adventure. Have you ever been to Vegas?"

"No."

"Then you're in for a treat, a slice of true western Americana. The Mirage brags about having a casino as big as a football field. Hookers are running around in hot pants. Cocktail waitresses serve free drinks to the gamblers under giant chandeliers the gamblers paid for. Old ladies with blue hair wearing white cotton gloves feed nickels into slot machines out of paper cups. The rooms are decorated in what one gambler calls 'early Sodom and Gomorrah,' and rich women sit at the blackjack tables in mink capes and stoles although outside, as another gambler put it, 'the heat would bring a Bedouin to his knees.' "

"And you *go* there?"

"I love it! It's a rare place! It's such a refreshing change from LAU and Evan Brodhead. Besides, I usually win money."

"Are you planning to gamble this time?"

"Oh, yes. That's how I'm going to get into Tally's office."

"I don't get it."

"Let it be a surprise. I think it'll work if I have to do it. I've still got to phone Akira, and then I think we'd better get some sleep. Will you be okay?"

"I'm okay. Good night, then."

He gave her a hug and a warm kiss. "Good night, sweetheart."

She eyed him speculatively as she moved off.

He picked up the phone.

"Can't you ever call before ten?" said Akira. "Don't you ever go to bed?"

"Not while the grown-ups are still having fun."

He briefed Akira on the evening's entertainment and asked if he'd drop by in the morning to pick up the report Mona typed.

"Sure. I'll wear my bulletproof vest."

Cliff showered and climbed into bed. He was tempted to read some Kahlil Gibran as a soporific but took up Wodehouse's *The Wooing of Archibald* instead, at the risk of losing sleep. He was well into it when he heard a knock at his bedroom door.

"Who is it?"

"What do you mean, 'Who is it?' " came a muffled voice through the wood. "Can I come in or not?"

"Sure. Come on in."

Mona opened the door and stalked in, wearing a terrycloth robe over a light green nightdress. She looked both fearful and determined.

"What's the matter? Are you okay?"

"I'm *not* okay! I'm scared and lonesome in there."

"Oh. Well . . ." He put the Wodehouse aside.

"I'm going to ask you one of my famous blunt questions,

Clifford Dunbar. Are you, or are you not, in love with me?"

His heart leaped.

"I am. I am! I love you, Mona! I absolutely adore you!"

"Well, I'm crazy in love with you, so why don't we go to bed together, for God's sake, like any normal couple in this decadent age?"

He turned off the light, rose, and took Mona in his arms in a long and warm embrace. They put aside their nightclothes and embraced again, naked, floating, ecstatic.

Mona slipped into bed, and Cliff followed.

"Viens plus près, mon amour," he murmured.

"Ton coeur contre mon coeur," she responded.

FIFTEEN

When Akira Yonenaka saw them sitting together in the breakfast nook the next morning, he knew exactly how things stood.

"I'm glad to see you two are hitting it off," he observed. "I know it's tough, two people living at close quarters."

"I think I like you better when you're impassive," said Cliff.

"Don't be stuffy, Cliff," said Mona. "Yes, Akira, we've decided we're fond of each other."

"I'm happy for both of you. Where's the report?"

"Right here. I want to give you two copies, one for you to keep, and one—well, Mona and I are going to Vegas this afternoon, and we may or may not run into trouble. If we do, give a copy to Lieutenant Puterbaugh. Otherwise, just hold it for me."

"Sure. Glad I can help."

"It's your chance to be useful as well as Oriental."

"Funny—but I've heard that one before."

They boarded their PSA flight at Burbank Airport along with a straggling double column of eager gamblers. In the seats just in front of them an old crapshooter was coaching a younger man, advising him to start off by sticking to bets on the pass line and come box, and place bets on six and eight. Several people studied racing forms. A pretty college girl had put her cosmetics case on her lap and was rapidly running through a deck of cards, snapping them down two at a time and glancing at her wristwatch.

"What on earth is she doing?" asked Mona.

"Casing a deck—counting down the values of the cards.

She's a blackjack player. I've seen her before, and she's good."

"What *is* counting?"

"You're trying to get a higher hand than the dealer without busting—going over twenty-one—right? So the more high cards that are left in the deck as the game goes on, the better your chances. You want lots of aces, face cards, tens, and nines, so it's to your advantage every time a small card is dealt and gotten rid of."

"So if the deck is half gone and there are lots of tens and aces, you start betting more money?"

"Exactly. In the system Phil Fixico taught me, an eight counts zero—it's neutral. Two and seven count plus one; three, four, and six are plus two; a five is plus three. When the big cards are gone, you're at a disadvantage, so nine is minus one, tens and face cards are minus two, and aces are minus three."

"And people sit there and do all that arithmetic in their heads?"

"It's even more complex than that, but that's the idea."

"I think I'd rather hang wallpaper."

Cliff laughed. "You're smart. Well, I'm a card counter, but not as good as Fixico."

In a scant fifty minutes the plane flew past the last burned brown hills west of Las Vegas and descended to the sandy desert floor at McCarran Airport. The great hotels and casinos, clustered like the pipes of an organ, shot up from the desert floor: Hilton International, MGM Grand, Maxim, Landmark, Caesar's Palace, the Dunes, the Mirage, a dozen others.

People scrambled for taxis and limousines in the blistering heat, but Mona and Cliff, with no baggage to wait for, beat them all. Their cab rolled down the Vegas Strip, which seemed to consist alternately of casinos and sandy, empty lots, possibly the most expensive worthless land in the United States. A peacock would have felt shabby next to the towering, elaborate, free-standing signs studded with thousands of light bulbs and neon tubes.

They reached welcome shade when the cabbie turned off the Strip and deposited them under the giant porte-cochere of the Mirage. They mounted the steps and went through the double set of automatic doors into the lobby, where the temperature instantly dropped thirty degrees.

In front of them, down a flight of red-carpeted steps, stretched the famed casino, a great green football field with rows of green-covered blackjack and craps tables, among which people wandered looking for the lucky spot. A metallic army of slot machines extended in military ranks to the left of the gaming tables as far as the eye could see. Lights twinkled everywhere: red, blue, yellow, green, amber, pink. Cards flashed white on the blackjack tables. A girl in a tiny red uniform, the panties hitched up so tight in the crotch they nearly lifted her off the floor, hurried past, the word "KENO" on her back in black letters. From a distant craps table a shooter screamed, *"Ee-yo-leven!"*

"Un-be-lievable!" said Mona.

"You'll get used to it."

A courteous desk clerk directed them to Pellegrino's office on executive row at the rear of the casino. They entered the reception room, which was furnished with very plausible-looking Louis Quinze antiques. The walls bore a few framed certificates and dozens of autographed pictures of movie stars.

A lovely young woman with hair like a skein of raw silk, wearing a simple black dress and a string of cultured pearls, sat at a neat desk behind a walnut railing.

"May I help you?" she inquired with a charming smile.

"I'd like to see Mr. Pellegrino."

"Do you have an appointment?"

"No, I was just dropping by."

"And may I ask the nature of your business?"

"It's very personal—and very important. I'm sure he'll want to see me."

"What is your name, please?"

"Clifford Dunbar. And this is Miss Moore."

"Oh! . . . Just a moment. I'll, uh, see if he's in."

"You mean you don't know?" said Cliff.

The subtle accusation seemed to wound her. "Mr. Pellegrino has another exit door in his office that he sometimes uses."

She went in and closed the door but was not gone for long. She overflowed with regret when she reappeared. "He doesn't seem to be here," she said. "But when you telephoned recently, Mr. Pellegrino *did* inform me that he doesn't know you and"— with a whaddaya-gonna-do-gesture —"prefers to keep it that way. However," she added, applying lotion to the burn, "if you'll leave your card I'm *sure* he'll call you when he gets the chance."

"If he should happen to come back in the next fifteen or twenty seconds, I have some papers here that will fascinate him."

"Would you care to leave them with me?"

"I'd rather not. You'll be seeing him soon, won't you?"

"I never know."

"All right. I'll try again later."

"Please do that. But I wouldn't get my hopes up."

Out in the hall Mona said, "Now what?"

"Gambit No. 2. As Chaucer said, it's a poor mouse that has but one hole to run to."

He led her into the casino and along a row of blackjack tables until he found a twenty-five-dollar-minimum table with only one player sitting at it, in the center seat.

"Take third base, hon, and I'll sit here," he said loudly.

Cliff slid into the second seat from the end to the dealer's right, leaving an empty stool between himself and the other player. Mona sat at the end to the far right of the dealer, whose name tag identified him as Roy.

Cliff took five hundred-dollar bills from his wallet and tossed them on the table. "Make it all quarters, Roy."

Roy laid the five bills side by side so that watchers in the Eye in the Sky could see them and called over his shoulder to the pit boss, "Five hundred!"

The pit boss glanced at the bills and nodded. Roy laid them crosswise over a slot in the table and pushed them in with a short board. He deftly laid out four stacks of five green chips each, put them together in two stacks of ten, and pushed them over to Cliff.

"Is the lady playing?"

"No."

Cliff placed a single green chip on the small rectangle printed at his position as Roy shuffled the two decks he was dealing.

Cliff consistently bet one chip on each hand all the way through the two decks, winning a few hands, losing a few more, as the count wandered up and down between positive and negative. His lis moved slightly and he stared intently, frowning, as Roy dealt all the cards face up except for the dealer's hole card. The count dropped steadily—minus ten, seventeen, twenty. At the end of the two decks, Cliff was down seven chips.

Roy shuffled. The count went only shallowly negative at first, and Cliff won as many hands as he lost. He kept his gaze on the cards. The next several hands contained a short flurry of threes, fives, sixes, and sevens and went mildly positive. Cliff smiled at Roy and put out two chips and won. Roy began to take an interest in him, which grew as the count rose steadily and Cliff won about three of every four hands with two chips bet on each one.

When Roy shuffled again, Cliff was nine chips to the good— two hundred twenty-five dollars.

Cliff put out two chips for the opening hand of the new deal and won. Although the count rose steadily in his favor, he continued to bet only two chips per hand. When the count reached plus twenty-two in the middle of the deck, Cliff suddenly put out a stack of six chips for the next hand, with a pleased little smile. Roy's eyebrows twitched. He remained deadpan but must have made some undetectable sign to the pit boss.

The pit boss, pacing slowly up and down between two rows

of tables, paused nearby and casually turned his attention to Table B-12, where Cliff sat with his six-chip bet. The pit boss was a stout, balding man with a neatly trimmed fringe of graying hair and a wide lower jaw with moist, fat lips. He could have been taken for a Presbyterian minister had he not been wearing a sports jacket that appeared to have been tailored from one of the gaudier patterns of automobile upholstery.

As he watched, with folded arms, Roy dealt a ten and a six to the other player, a five and a four to Cliff, and a six for himself on top of his face-down hole card. That made the count twenty-nine in Cliff's system. The other player stood pat on his sixteen. Cliff doubled his bet, putting out another stack of six chips and sliding his two cards, overlapped, under his bet. The dealer turned up his hole card, a nine, dealt himself an eight, and busted. He paid off the other player and pushed twelve chips over to Cliff. The pit boss sucked in his lips.

The count was still a fat plus twenty-eight. Looking very pleased indeed, Cliff shoved a stack of twelve chips onto the betting spot. The pit boss unfolded his arms and took a step nearer.

Roy dealt the other player a nineteen, a pair of eights to Cliff, and an up-card of seven to himself. The other player stood. Cliff split the eights and put an additional twelve chips on the second eight. He was now playing two hands. Roy dealt him an ace to go with the first eight; Cliff stood on the resulting nineteen. Roy dealt him yet another eight, and Cliff split that one out and put twelve more chips by it. He was now playing three hands. Roy gave him a queen on the second eight and a ten on the third one. Cliff stood on his nineteen and two eighteens. Roy turned up his hole card—a ten—for a losing seventeen.

"Nice going," said the other player.

"That *was* all right, wasn't it?" said a delighted Cliff.

Sourly, Roy pushed thirty-six green chips over to Cliff. He had won nine hundred dollars on a single round.

The pit boss moved in quickly beside the dealer and said to Cliff in polite tones backed up by massive weight, "Sir, I'm going to have to ask you not to play blackjack here anymore."

Cliff looked up in surprise. "Why? Just because I won?"

"I know what you're doing."

"I don't understand you!"

"I know what you're doing."

"I don't get it! What do you think I'm doing?"

"Sir, you are welcome to play any other game in the house—craps, baccarat, roulette, poker, but not blackjack."

"You mean you are barring me from all blackjack tables?"

"That is absolutely correct."

"Well, this is an outrage! Wait a minute—I get it—you think I'm a card counter, don't you?"

"Sir, I am only saying you are welcome to play any other game in the house."

"What if I don't want to play any other game?"

"Then you'll have to go to another casino."

"And what if I don't want to go to another casino?"

"Look, sir, do you want me to call a security guard and have you shown out?"

"You try that and some people are going to be very unhappy!"

"Who, for instance?"

"Tally Pellegrino, for one!"

They stared levelly at each other.

"You know Tally Pellegrino?"

"I do."

"And what is your name, sir?"

"Find out for yourself!"

"I intend to do that, sir. Stay right where you are."

The pit boss picked up the phone at his desk and said something Cliff could not hear, beyond "Tally? Marty at B-12 . . ."

The pit boss returned to the table and stood with folded arms, glaring at Cliff, who glared back.

Within two minutes, a man appeared at Cliff's side, well

dressed and well groomed. He was fairly short, about five-seven, but carried himself like Julius Caesar. He was slim, tan, with curly black hair and dark brown eyes that flickered with intelligence. He wore a navy blue blazer with white buttons, gray slacks, polished black moccasins, and a flat gold wristwatch with no numerals. That last touch was consonant with the environment. There are no clocks in Las Vegas casinos.

The other player had left long since, play having come to a halt at Table B-12. Pellegrino looked at Cliff and raised his eyebrows inquiringly. The pit boss nodded.

"You know this gentleman?" asked the pit boss.

"I haven't had the pleasure. What seems to be your trouble, sir?"

"I'm Clifford Dunbar."

Pellegrino narrowed his eyes and expelled air through his teeth. "Je-sus Christ!"

"Want him out, Tally?"

"No, it's okay, Marty. I'll handle it. All right, Dunbar. I give up. Come on back to my office."

Roy gave Cliff a stack of black hundred-dollar chips, which he dropped into his jacket pocket. He and Mona followed Pellegrino back through the slot machines to his office. The secretary shot them a smile-to-cover-any-occasion as they came in and disappeared into Pellegrino's sanctum.

"Okay, Dunbar, what's on your mind?"

"You'll be interested in something I wrote. Mona?"

She handed him the summary on the *Bay Psalm Book* case. Cliff passed it to Pellegrino, who glanced at the title page and the first paragraph.

"Listen, I know what the *Bay Psalm Book* is. Perry Winthrop gave it to LAU. So why bring this paper to Las Vegas—to a *casino*, for God's sake? You want us to pass it around the crap tables?"

"Winthrop is a business associate of yours in a small way. I'm sure you wish him luck in the election. But he isn't going to win the election. The book is a forgery, and I'm going to expose it. What's more, Winthrop knew it was a forgery all along, and I'm going to prove that. The IRS is going to disqualify his tax deduction, and to cap it off, this forgery is connected in some way, direct or indirect, with the murder of a friend of mine. I don't know how, yet, but I'm going to nail that down too. Also, two thugs tried to knife *me* in a parking lot because I was on to this scheme."

"Who were they?" said Pellegrino sharply.

"A couple of hired killers—"

Pellegrino's eyes glittered.

"—young punks in their twenties."

Pellegrino kept his eyes steady, unblinking.

"This is all very interesting, but why fly to Vegas to tell *me* about it?"

"Let's say it's because I'm not Sylvester Stallone."

"I don't get you. But okay, I'll look at your paper."

"You can skip over most of the technical stuff, but you might want to read page one and pages nine and ten."

He did so, glancing up at Cliff occasionally with something resembling the respect of one battle-toughened heavyweight for another. When he finished he stacked the sheets neatly on his desk.

"Reads like *True Detective*. Mind if I keep this?"

"Be my guest."

"Have you shown this to the cops?"

"Not yet, but a friend of mine is holding a copy to give to the West Los Angeles Division—in case."

Pellegrino leaned one elbow on his desk and tapped a canine tooth with a fingernail, gazing thoughtfully at a corner of the ceiling. Then his face froze and he banged his fist.

"*Stronzo!*"

"What?"

"Winthrop—the son-of-a-bitch! At the start, he told us the book was real! You're right, Dunbar, we've been backing the wrong horse, but no more. As of tomorrow there'll be no connection between him and the Mirage Hotel."

"You're going to buy back his interest?"

"Buy back, shit! Excuse me, lady."

" 'Sokay," said Mona. "I've heard the word."

"Go on back to L.A., you two." Turning to Cliff, he added, "And don't worry about a thing."

"Thanks, Tally."

Cliff and Mona made for the door.

"Hey, Dunbar!"

Cliff turned.

"No blackjack on the way out! You're eighty-sixed!"

Cliff grinned and closed the door behind him.

They went the the cashier's cage, where Cliff cashed in his chips: seventeen blacks and two greens—seventeen hundred fifty dollars, for a net win of twelve hundred fifty.

In the cab on the way to the airport Mona said, "You may like it, but I never want to see this place again! It's unclean!"

"What are you talking about? I think this has been a very profitable trip!"

SIXTEEN

When he awoke the next morning, Cliff realized he was living in an earthly paradise. He lay on his back in his dream house, in the quietude, his eyes on the ceiling, where bands of green light undulated gently to and fro like the waters in a Hawaiian tide pool. He turned his eyes toward the window. A light breeze stirred the long leaves of the banana trees outside, green rainbows that let only green light through. And beside him lay Mona, breathing quietly, her dandelion hair framing her placid face with its pert profile and sprinkling of freckles.

Marvelous. . . . Marvell . . . Andrew Marvell. Yes, those lines in *The Garden*, about the creative mind "annihilating all that's made to a green thought in a green shade." And those oranges in *Bermudas*, "Like golden lamps in a green night." And best of all, he thought, looking lovingly at Mona's sleeping face, those powerful lines at the end of *To His Coy Mistress*:

> Let us roll all our strength, and all
> Our sweetness, up into one ball:
> And tear our pleasures with rough strife,
> Through the iron gates of life.

They had done just that.

"Mona . . . Mona . . . sweetheart."

"Yes, darling?"

"Are you awake enough to answer a question?"

"Mm-hm."

"Open your eyes so I'll know."

She opened her eyes. "Oh, how beautiful!"

"What is?"

"The wavy green light on the ceiling."

"It is, isn't it? It comes through the banana trees."

"What's your question?"

"Will you marry me?"

"You mean I'm that good a lay?"

"*Mona*—that is *unseemly*!"

She laughed mischievously. "Shocked you again, didn't I?"

"I'm *trying* to be *romantic*!"

"And you are. Probably much more than you realize. You darling man, under that *macho* exterior you're a sweet, sentimental fuff."

"How about a serious answer to my question?"

"I'm sorry. I think we'd better start over. Besides, I want to hear it again. Ask me again, and I promise to behave myself."

"Will you marry me?"

"Yes. Yes. I will marry you, and I will love you forever as I love you now."

She twined her arms around his neck and they joined in a long kiss. When they parted, Mona said, "Sorry about my breath. I always have bad breath in the morning."

"I don't care. 'A friend should bear his friend's infirmities.' "

"That's very nice."

"Shakespeare. Brutus and Cassius."

"Which one had the bad breath?"

The telephone rang.

"Well, of all the inopportune times!" grumbled Cliff, rolling over to answer it.

"Why answer it?"

He paused as it rang again. "I have to answer it."

"Who says? God?"

"You have to answer the phone."

"Not me. When the phone rings, somebody is asking permission to talk to me. If I don't feel like talking, I don't answer it."

He picked up the phone.

"Conformist!" said Mona, stroking his cheek.

"Dr. Dunbar? This is Perry Winthrop. I'm so glad I caught you at home."

"I'm always at home at six-thirty in the morning."

"Oh, did I wake you? If I did I'm—I'm sorry."

"No, I was already awake."

"It's imperative that I see you at once. That is—if it will be convenient for you."

"Sure. Come on over. Do you have my address?"

"Oh, yes, Fred Collins gave it to me. Would—how about nine o'clock? Would that be too early?"

"Nine o'clock's fine."

"Splendid! I'll see you then, and thank you."

Cliff hung up the phone. "That was Perry Winthrop."

"I thought so."

"He sounded rattled. I would guess Tally Pellegrino has eighty-sixed him, too."

"Well, let's crawl out of bed like two good American fiancés and have a decent breakfast before he gets here."

The doorbell rang at exactly nine o'clock. Cliff examined him through the peephole. Winthrop looked reasonably well groomed in his gray suit and vest, white-on-white shirt, blue tie, and gold cufflinks, but he looked a trifle gritty around the eyes, and he had shaven none too well. He had a red nick below one sideburn, too, where he had dug in too hastily with his razor. He was staring at Cliff's front door with a puzzled look that persisted after Cliff opened it.

"Good morning," said Cliff. "Come in."

"Who did that to your door?"

"Two Gentlemen of Verona."

Winthrop shook his head but inquired no further. Cliff ushered him into the library, where he sat stiffly with his hands on his knees. Mona followed and seated herself to one side.

"I'm sure you're wondering why I'm here."

"You got a call yesterday from Tally Pellegrino."

Winthrop was too worried to feel surprised.

"He canceled two contracts," Cliff went on. "One with you—and one with me."

"I'm just as glad. I feel just a little bit cleaner, not having shady people among my political backers."

"You mean Fred Collins and Floretta Bishop have quit, too?"

Winthrop was startled. "Why, no. Why should they?"

"Surely you know that Floretta was a whorehouse madam who shot and killed a gangster, and cousin Fred defended her."

"Floretta may be *for* me, but she isn't a backer. And Fred's a lawyer. He defended her, as is legal and proper, and she was acquitted. Let's not assign guilt by association."

"Isn't it a strange association that Floretta should have been almost on the spot when Link Schofield was killed?"

"It's a strange coincidence, surely—but just a coincidence."

"Maybe."

"But this is all far afield from the reason I came to see you." He looked down at his hands, frowned, and heaved a heavy sigh.

"Dr. Dunbar, you're quite right. The *Bay Psalm Book* is a forgery." He looked up at Cliff. "And I have come to throw myself completely on your mercy. In all humility, I beg you not to expose the book until after the election."

"Where did you get the book?"

"Loren Brewner brought it to me quite a while back."

"And he knew it was a forgery?"

"He did it himself."

"Why?"

"He originally set out to publish a facsimile edition. He had an early-seventeenth-century font from the same typefounder who made Stephen Daye's font. He was going to propose that the Huntington Library fund the facsimile project, but then the printing started to look so authentic to him that he decided to see if he could carry it off—create a replica—paper, text, and all."

"I have to hand it to him, he did an incredible job."

"Until you and this young lady"—he gave Mona a wan smile—"put it under a magnifying glass."

"Why did he bring it to you?"

"He had done printing for me before. And he is—well, you might say an avid supporter of mine."

"I know. Almost a fanatic."

"And he knew how strapped I was for money."

"I thought you were a millionaire."

"I was at one time, but I had a few losses and I spent a good deal of money on election campaigns in Massachusetts—and then for this campaign, I had to liquidate almost all of my remaining income-producing assets."

"What do you mean, you *had* to?"

"Part of it was my own doing. This was my last golden opportunity to move up to an important political position, and I was willing to stake my all on it. And besides, well— certain of my supporters were willing to back me financially only on condition that I commit my own money as well. They wanted to make certain I'd go all out and not leave them stuck with the whole check, as it were."

"Which supporters were those?"

Winthrop squirmed and hitched himself sideways in his chair. "Mainly, uh, my Las Vegas constituents."

"Uh-huh. I would guess they also wanted to see you broke, so you'd be more likely to play ball according to their rules."

"Oh, there's no denying that tit-for-tat is part of the political game, but I assure you I had no intention of just selling out my principles—and I made that clear to them in no uncertain terms."

"No doubt."

"However, there's also no denying that being extremely short of funds hampers an officeholder's latitude of action. So I'm afraid I clutched at the drowning man's straw when

Brewner told me the book would be worth upward of a quarter of a million if it could pass critical scrutiny."

"Why on earth didn't you just sell it outright, then, or put it on the block at a booksellers' auction?"

"I thought it would be safer tucked away in an academic library and out of the commercial market. That way, even if the forgery were detected, I wouldn't have somebody suddenly demanding that I restore three hundred thousand dollars I didn't have. I could simply take the book back. Meanwhile, I could claim my contribution as a tax deduction."

"I don't get that. That wouldn't bring you any money."

"Indirectly it would, and it did. It enabled me to keep many tens of thousands of dollars I otherwise would have had to pay in taxes this year, and it will do the same for me in the next couple of years. You see," he said, warming to a happier subject, "the IRS lets you claim that sort of deduction to an amount up to half of your year's income. And if it's a large contribution like this one, that exceeds half your income, they let you carry the excess forward. Mind you, my capital gains when I liquidated were nothing like six hundred thousand dollars, but they were sizable. And my future carry-over deductions would help me greatly in rebuilding my fortunes."

"But isn't there some legal limitation on how much of your own money you can put in your campaign?"

"Not in California. There is in New York."

"Helps to be a lawyer, doesn't it?"

"Sometimes," he replied with a tired smile. "So when Bradford Silliman and C. T. Post authenticated it, I thought I was home free. I will still be free if you will kindly consent to wait a few months. No—I won't attempt to bribe you again. I will merely leave it to your generosity."

"And why do you think I should be so generous?"

"Two reasons. Dr. Dunbar, I've been in politics most of my life. I'm a public servant with a definite political philosophy—a set of high principles I strongly believe in. Perhaps you disagree with them, I don't know. But I am convinced I would be an effective governor of this state. I believe I can do a great deal for California, and I don't believe I should be deprived of the opportunity to be of great public service because of what amounts to a little white lie that hurt no one."

"What's the second reason?"

"It's less important—but it's to save my life. I mean that quite literally."

Winthrop clasped his hands together and leaned forward, his eyes burning with intensity.

"I am in a desperate situation, Dr. Dunbar. The exposure of that book would mean my utter ruination. It would leave me worse than penniless, it would leave me in debt. If I had to take the book back, the IRS would of course disallow my deduction and demand money that I flatly would not have. And it would cost me the election—especially if the public even faintly suspected that I had anything to do with your friend's murder. The public is always ready to suspect the worst of politicians. You know: 'Where there's smoke there's fire'? It would also ruin my good name. I am the last of my branch of the Winthrop line, which has been a distinguished American family. My life would be over at the age of fifty-nine. I would see no other recourse than just to—end it all."

"Nonsense. You wouldn't do that. Not with your ego."

"I just might."

"And it's ridiculous to say your life would be over. There are many things you could still do."

"I don't see what."

"You can practice law, for heaven's sake! Unless you're disbarred, which I think very unlikely."

"Practice law?"

"Why not? You might even turn into an honest man again."

"Oh, now, just a moment!"

"Listen, Winthrop, a minute ago you argued against guilt by association. But my God, man, take a good *look* at your associates: a forger, the Mafia, a Mafia mouthpiece—and, secondhand, I grant you, a whorehouse madam."

"Don't forget I have other backers. However, the old saying is true that politics make strange bedfellows."

"I know, but you got yourself involved in a grubby daisy chain. And somewhere in that motley crew is the person who killed Link Schofield and tried to have me knifed in a parking lot! And that front door was shot up by a couple of hoods who tried to get me again. And now you have the colossal gall to ask me to behave like Elsie the Borden Cow and fill a bucket with the milk of human kindness!"

"I know. And you're quite justified in being miffed."

"*Miffed*!" Mona exploded.

Winthrop jumped. He apparently had forgotten she was there.

"People try to murder him twice and you call him miffed!"

"It was an unfortunate choice of words."

"And I was scared spitless because I could have been shot up with him. We were both *enraged*—when we got over the shakes!"

"I can't tell you how sorry I am about these acts of violence. I assure you I had nothing to do with them."

"Oh, no?" said Mona. "Let me ask you a couple of questions. You have nothing to hide, right?"

"No, not a thing."

"Then what did Lincoln Schofield really want when he came to see you that afternoon?"

Winthrop lowered his eyes and worked his jaw.

"Confession is good for the soul, Mr. Winthrop."

"He came to tell me the book was a forgery. He found what he claimed were typographic discrepancies. He suggested I withdraw my donation."

"And what did you say?"

"What could I say? I had to deny it, of course. I was in far too deep. I told him Silliman and Post were sufficient authorities for me."

"And he left?"

"Yes."

"And you panicked?"

"I was very upset, of course."

"And who did you tell about this?"

"Miss Moore, I see what you're driving at, but I swear on my word of honor I did not arrange any sort of assault on Mr. Schofield. I could never do such a thing."

"Maybe not, but even a few Presidents have been known to sort of say to underlings, 'You guys decide among yourselves how to handle this—but I don't want to know anything about it.'"

"I didn't even do that, Miss Moore."

"No," said Cliff. "But you didn't answer Mona's question. Who did you tell?"

"My close associates, of course. I warned Brewner, too, naturally."

"But not Tally Pellegrino?"

"Oh, lord, no!"

"Did you ask people for ideas on what to do?"

"Oh, I'm sure I did that. And I suppose it's possible that some overzealous supporter took it upon himself to . . . to . . . Dr. Dunbar, did you see that movie with O'Toole and Burton about Henry II and Thomas à Becket?"

"No, but I read the book."

"Do you remember that scene where Henry is all wrought up and says something like, 'Will no one rid me of this turbulent priest?' And two knights went straight to the cathedral and killed him and Henry felt simply terrible about it because Becket was his friend? Well, that's how I felt when I heard of the attack on Schofield. I can't tell you how appalled I was."

"But you don't know who did it?"

"I haven't the faintest idea."

"From what you say, though, it almost had to be Collins or Brewner—or both—or people they hired. And we're also back to Floretta again."

"It still could have been two random hoodlums, too."

"I doubt it, with Floretta on the scene."

"Mr. Winthrop," said Mona, "at some point you must have told Tally Pellegrino the book was a forgery and we were onto it, or he wouldn't have had two hoods shoot up the front door."

"I don't deny that. I had to tell him when the situation got really threatening."

"But you didn't suggest he lean on me?" said Cliff.

"Certainly not."

"You just dropped an innuendo here and an innuendo there and then removed yourself gracefully with your self-esteem intact."

"I'm not as hypocritical as all that."

"Nonetheless, somehow I got knifed and shot at in the aftermath."

"We seem to be talking at cross-purposes, Dr. Dunbar. I realize that you're absorbed in trying to solve the murder of your friend—understandably—whereas I'm concentrating all my energies on my campaign. I wish you luck in your task, and I would deeply appreciate your wishing me luck in mine. I wouldn't dream of asking you to drop your inquiry. I am here merely to put myself at your feet and ask—humbly—that you not ruin my career with a premature exposure of the book."

Cliff could scarcely believe his ears. "Winthrop, you're incredible! Do you really not see that the book and the murder are like Siamese twins joined at the heart? You can't simply ignore one of them, nor can you separate the two."

"I don't see why not."

"Then let me put it in Bobbsey Twins language. Let's say I'm convinced I've found the murderer. I tell the police. The police say, 'Why do you think he or she did it?' 'In order,' I say, 'to prevent exposing the *Bay Psalm Book* as a fake.' They say, 'You mean the book Perry Winthrop gave to LAU?' 'Yes,' I say. 'Crikey!' they say. 'Then that means Winthrop is a liar and a probable accessory to murder and can't win his election. We better look into this.' You see, Winthrop? It all comes in one string. I can't postpone my findings about the book without postponing my search for Link's killer."

"Then you won't do it?"

"No. Never."

"Then I will simply have to—do away with myself."

"That's up to you. But I hope you won't."

Winthrop slumped in his chair and closed his eyes.

"You think I'm an evil man, don't you?"

"Not consciously. But when you supped with the devil, you forgot to bring your long spoon."

Winthrop rose wearily from the chair and trudged to the front door with his head down. With his hand on the knob, however, he straightened up and said, turning, "I still think I would have made a good governor."

He went out, closing the door softly behind him.

"That poor man!" said Mona. "I feel sorry for him. He's a master of self-deception, but he told us a lot, didn't he?"

"Enough to make me realize I've taken things as far as I can. It's time to turn this over to the police. And I don't think Lieutenant Puterbaugh is going to be happy with me."

SEVENTEEN

*H*e was right. Puterbaugh was miffed.

"Goddamn it, Dunbar, I ought to have you jugged for withholding evidence! Who the hell do you think you are, Fearless Fosdick?"

"I came in when I knew I had something."

"Sure, after you've been dicking around and damn near got yourself killed and stuck me with *your* murder! And then I'm supposed to go after the Mafia? Jesus!"

"Lieutenant, be reasonable. What if I'd come running in here all breathless with my tongue hanging out and said, 'Guess what, Puterbaugh—the *Bay Psalm Book* has two typos in it!' How would you have reacted? Would you have called out a SWAT team?"

Puterbaugh rubbed his bald scalp, and his eyes snapped.

"You could have filled me in right after Flett and Peasoup went for you in the parking lot."

"I didn't know anything then. All I had were vague suspicions. Everything hinged on whether the book was a forgery, and it took bibliographers and a proofreader to decide that, not police."

"We've got a crime lab. And we could have given you police protection after those two hoods shot up your place. *If* you had reported it."

"For how long? Three days? A week? The Mafia had a contract out on me, you know."

"All right, all right! What a week. I wish something nice would happen to me for a change."

"I see you won another bowling trophy."

"Yeah."

Two bowlers were now frozen in time and space atop Puterbaugh's filing cabinet.

"Have you got a private investigator's license?"

"No."

"Well, get one, if you're going to do any more of this kind of work. At least you'll be legit, and I can have you busted when you get out of line."

"No more for me. This bibliography is too racy a life for me."

"That goes for proofreading, too," said Mona. "All I want now is to go fishing—and get married."

"To him?"

"Mm-hm."

"Congratulations. You'll lead a very exciting life. Dunbar—have you told me everything you know? I constantly get the feeling around you that you're always holding out."

"I've given you my all. Scout's honor."

"How about those two hoods? They shoot up your place, they run off, and you hightail it straight to Vegas. How did you know they were Mafia?"

"They wore hats and they had tomato-paste stains on their shirts."

"Shit! Sorry, lady."

" 'Sokay."

Puterbaugh sighed. "Okay, Dunbar, I've got your report. What do you expect us to do with it?"

"Hang onto it, mainly. It's like an insurance policy for me. However, I brought along a brochure I picked up in Loren Brewner's print shop. It has a good halftone photo of Brewner in it. I suggest you show it to Flett and see if he identifies Brewner as the one who hired him. Twist his arm—tell him the jig is up—hint at plea-bargaining if you have to."

"Gee, thanks! I would never have thought of that!"

"Sorry. But I also think you should dig up pictures of Fred Collins and Floretta Bishop and show him those, too."

"Gee whillikers! Maybe I'll do just that!"

"I apologize, Lieutenant. I've been so absorbed in this case that I've come to regard it as mine-all-mine."

"Yeah. Well, you did a fantastic job. We could have cooperated, though. And now, get your ass out of here, Fosdick. Sorry, lady."

"That's all right. I'm getting mine out, too."

The phone rang at nine the next morning. Mona answered.

"Miss Moore? Lieutenant Puterbaugh. Is Fosdick there?"

"Just a moment. . . . Fearless, dear! It's for you."

He gave her a light blow on top of the head and took the phone.

"Dunbar? We've won round one. I confronted Flett with Brewner's picture yesterday afternoon."

"And he identified him?"

"Not right away. He denied everything and stalled around until I told him we had a warrant out for Brewner's arrest."

"And did you?"

"No, but I do now. I told Flett if he opened up I could arrange to have him indicted on a simple assault charge. If he waited till we brought Brewner in, they would both be tried for assault with intent to commit murder, conspiracy to commit murder, attempted murder, and solicitation of a felony. If he was very lucky, he'd get out of Folsom in the year 2000."

"So he sang?"

"A regular Luciano Pavarotti."

"How about Lincoln Schofield's murder?"

"He denied up, down, and sideways that he had anything to do with it."

"Do you believe him?"

"Who knows? He sounded convincing, but so would you if you were facing a murder rap."

"Have you arrested Brewner yet?"

"Give me time, will you? I've hardly finished my danish.

Sergeant Garth and I are going over to South Pasadena now. I've also got a search warrant. How would you like to come along as an expert in case we find the plates or whatever you call 'em that he printed that book with? Okay? Pick you up in forty-five minutes."

They parked in the yellow loading zone directly in front of the shop on Division Street. Puterbaugh and Sergeant Garth entered first, while Cliff trailed behind. No one was at the desk. Puterbaugh banged the little bell. No answer. He rang it several times.

There still being no answer, Puterbaugh lifted the hinged gate in the counter and was about to pass through when a large, fat, pink-faced young man with sleepy eyes appeared in the doorway behind the counter carrying a plastic photoreduction wheel. The eyes woke up when he saw Puterbaugh.

"Hey, no! Mr. Brewner'd shit a brick if he saw you doing that!"

"Where is Mr. Brewner?"

"Who are you?"

"Police. Where's Brewner?"

"Maybe out in the alley. I saw him go through the back doorway just a few seconds ago."

Puterbaugh and Garth dashed out the rear door of the shop. There was no sign of Brewner in the alley.

"What's going on? What do you want him for?"

"Quick! Is his car gone?"

At approximately the pace of an ox pulling a heavy plow through rain-soaked clay, the young man osmosed outside. "Yeah, it's gone. I know he was planning to go over to Tinker Graphics for some fountain solution."

"Jesus Christ! What kind of car does he drive?"

"A 1978 Maverick two-door. Green. Or is it blue? It was dusty most of the time."

"Do you know the license number?"

"I never noticed it."

"Sergeant, get on the radio and have 'em run a DMV check. You got Brewner's full name? And alert the local police. Stay on till you get that license number and then broadcast that."

Turning to the fat young man, Puterbaugh said, "Did he see us coming in?"

"Gee, I don't know. I was figurin' out how much to reduce an outsize chart to fit eight and a half by eleven when I heard him say, 'Oh, oh, back in a minute, Yates.' That's me. Joe Yates."

"You're all alone here?"

"Yeah, it's Saturday. I was helping Mr. Brewner with a special job. What's he done?"

"That can wait. Where's his office?"

"Up front on the right."

A locked door stood in the far wall of Brewner's office.

"Where does that door lead to?"

"Nowhere," said Yates. "Just a storeroom. Mr. Brewner keeps a lot of personal stuff in there."

"His collection of old type fonts?" asked Cliff.

"Some of 'em. He keeps some of 'em at home."

"Is there a key around?"

"Oh, God, no! Mr. Brewner always carried the key, and he said if he ever caught any of us fooling around in there, he'd stomp a mudhole in our ass. He's kind of a character!" Yates chuckled.

"In that case—" Puterbaugh kicked the door in.

Cliff's eye was instantly caught by an old yellow-oak cabinet with eighteen or twenty shallow drawers about three feet wide. He slid one open.

And there it was: the type for eight pages of the *Bay Psalm Book*, still neatly locked in the chase.

"Could you take an impression of one of these?" Cliff asked Yates. "Not a good one, just one that's legible."

"Sure thing."

Cliff opened drawers until he spotted "Psalme 23." He removed the chase and set it on a worktable. Yates inked the type with a roller, laid a sheet of paper on it, and went over it with another roller.

Cliff peeled off the sheet and read, on page E2, "The Lord to mee a shepherd is, want therefore shall not I. . . ." with the "a" missing from "shepheard."

EIGHTEEN

*T*he June Sunday was so glorious that even Goldina Fuller brought her bathing suit—a new one she had bought on Saturday because Saturday had been equally glorious.

"I resolved," said she to Cliff and Mona under the umbrella beside the pool, "that I was *not* going to come to a swimming party and inhibit everybody. So here I am, wrinkles, varicose veins, and all. I *may* even go swimming!"

"Goldina, you look terrific," said Mona.

"And that woman is a physical therapist," said Cliff.

"I'm serious," said Mona. "I only hope I look that good twenty years from now."

"Forty."

"You don't mean it."

"Very well, then, forty-five. Gracious! Who is that striking woman who just came out of the house? What a beautiful tan. Is she Italian?"

"No, that's Pearl Humphrey, Lincoln Schofield's daughter."

"Oh, dear! The poor girl!"

"And here comes Akira Yonenaka. He was Link's assistant."

"I'm his successor now," said Akira, coming up. "Just got the news: I'm not going to be stuck with the Oriental Center library."

"Congratulations! Akira, meet Goldina Fuller, famed sleuth and undercover agent."

Akira gave her a little bow. "I've been an admirer of your work."

"And I'm glad it's over. What's our next case, Clifford?"

"We haven't settled this one yet."

He introduced Pearl and Goldina to each other. "I'm surprised we haven't met before," said Pearl. "I visited my father fairly often in your apartment building."

"Where's Phil?" Cliff asked.

"He's coming," said Akira. "Had to shower first. Oh—here he is now."

Philip Fixico, in khaki trunks and Mexican leather sandals, with a towel over his shoulder, appeared on the pool deck. Straight, tall, and muscled, he could have passed for a Masai warrior—perhaps the more so because of the slight limp from his war wound. Cliff introduced him all around.

"My goodness!" said Goldina. "Black *is* beautiful!"

Phil grinned. "You're not so bad yourself, doll. Is she my date, Cliff?"

"I suppose I'll have to give her up, now that I have Mona."

"You two are engaged?" Pearl asked. "That's marvelous. Dad would have approved. He worried about you, Cliff."

Cliff frowned. "Pearl, I had hoped this swimming party would be to celebrate catching Link's killer or killers, but we're still at a dead end. Brewner is probably holed up somewhere in the Jim Bridger Wilderness by now—and anyway, it's likely that some of the other people around Winthrop were involved, too. Maybe all of them. I don't know what the answers are."

"I know *one* of 'em!" said Goldina. "You mark my words: When the dust settles on this whole to-do, you're going to find that high-class chippie Floretta Bishop was in it up to her ears!"

"Chippie?" inquired Phil.

"A hooker," Cliff explained. "Wouldn't be surprised if you're right, Goldina."

"How come we're all hunched under this umbrella?" said Akira. "Isn't anybody going swimming?"

"The reason," said Cliff, "is that seated around this table are five of the nicest people in Los Angeles."

"Six," said Pearl.

"Thanks. I was hoping someone would say that. However, you're right, Akira, so as host, I will start things rolling with a diving demonstration featuring my superb one-and-a-half gainer, plus or minus one fourth."

He strode to the diving board amid a patter of applause. He shifted his feet into position at the end of the board and extended his arms. "Got your cameras ready?"

Mona caught a glint of light up on the slope among the ivy and scattered pine trees. For a split second she thought the glint actually did come from a camera lens, but as the barrel of the carbine came up, she screamed.

"Cliff!"

He had no time to react to her scream, but twenty-three-hundredths of a second elapsed during the squeezing of the trigger and the first movements of his dive.

The carbine cracked. The bullet, one-hundredth of a second late, plowed across the back of his skull. Cliff dropped into the water, where a red rose bloomed around his head. The carbine cracked again, shattering a tile at the edge of the pool. Pearl and Goldina slid under the table, screaming.

Phil Fixico dived into the water and began pulling Cliff to the far side of the pool below the angle of fire over the wall. Gouts of water shot up from near-misses. Akira ran for the gate in the wall that opened onto the slope.

In the fastest thinking of her life, Mona ran to the side of the house—and turned the sprinklers on full force.

Arching jets of water soared in the air, screening the slope in blue-white mist, darkening the pine tree trunks, raining on the ivy.

Akira, dodging from one tree to another, saw a tall, gray-haired man frantically trying to wipe the lenses of his glasses on the front of his shirt. He raced forward through the spray, snatched the carbine from the intruder, and seized his arm in a policeman's come-along.

Fixico dragged Cliff out of the pool and up against the foot of the garden wall as Mona raced up with a towel.

"Phil! Do you think he's all right?"

"Think so. Think he's just knocked out."

Not seeing any bone splinters, Mona pressed the towel against the wound to stop the bleeding. Looking up, she saw Akira forcing the man through the gate and onto the pool deck, keeping his captive in front of him as he continued to bend the man's arm in a ferocious wristlock.

"My God!" Mona said. "It's the printer, Brewner. I saw his picture in the brochure Cliff had. Pearl!" she called. "Get on the phone and call Lieutenant Puterbaugh!"

Pearl ran for the house. Goldina emerged from under the table and collapsed into a chair.

By the time Lieutenant Puterbaugh and Sergeant Garth pulled into the driveway, Akira had put Brewner in the leather library chair that had received so much use from Collins, Calcavecchia, and Winthrop. Brewner sat sullen and impassive, blinking like an owl at noon, helpless without his glasses, which Mona had retrieved and put on Cliff's desk.

Cliff had recovered consciousness. He wore a large, thick bandage on the back of his head and doggedly refused to be taken to the UCLA emergency hospital. "No. I want to see how this comes out. Then I'll go."

"Sergeant Garth," said Puterbaugh, "turn on the tape recorder." After a few remarks for the record, Puterbaugh turned to Brewner. "Mr. Brewner, I'm going to ask you a few questions. According to the law, you do not have to answer them. You have the right to remain silent. You also have the right to consult an attorney before answering any questions. If you don't have an attorney, the court will appoint one to defend you. Do you wish to consult an attorney?"

"Hell, no. I consulted one before, and look at the mess the son-of-a-bitch got me into."

"Who are you referring to?"

"That bastard Fred Collins."

"Is that G. Frederick Collins, the aide to Perry Winthrop?"

"That's the one. Well, it's blown up in our faces."

"Mr. Brewner, I again want to remind you of your right to remain silent."

"I heard you the first time. How about giving me my glasses?"

Puterbaugh handed them to him.

"It's up to you, Mr. Brewner. But as you appear willing to talk, I'd like to ask you one major question that has me baffled: Why did you kill Lincoln Schofield—or arrange to have him killed?"

Cliff was astonished at this bold, anything-but-subtle thrust, and still more astonished when Brewer answered readily.

"Because he was going to expose the *Bay Psalm Book*. What do you think? He was going to ruin me. I'd never work for the Huntington again, or for anybody else. I'd have to go back to raising alfalfa. And he was going to ruin Winthrop's chances to become the only decent governor we've had since 1900."

"What did Fred Collins have to do with this?"

"He's the one who said Schofield had to be eliminated. That cousin of his—that Floretta Bishop—she's the one who had the contacts with Flett and Richardson."

Goldina shot a knowing glance at Cliff.

"Only they said I was the one who had to make the deal with them—so I'd be in it as much as they were. And like an asshole, I went along."

"Well, Mr. Brewner, like the situation with President Nixon and the tapes, a lot of people are going to wonder—in fact, *I* wonder—why you had Flett and Richardson leave the book by the body. Why didn't you have it destroyed?"

Brewner gritted his teeth and clenched his fists. After a long pause he blurted out, "Because the book is a goddamn masterpiece! I didn't want it to go to waste!"

"Where were you at the time of the murder?"

"Home watching the Dodgers on the TV."

"Why was Floretta Bishop on the scene? Wasn't that risky?"

"It was her idea. Mrs. Know-it-all. Make sure nothing

happened to the book and give the police fake identification of the suspects."

"What was Perry Winthrop's involvement?"

"Are you crazy? He'd never get involved in such a thing. He never even knew about it, and I'll lock horns with anybody who says he did."

"How about the *Bay Psalm Book*, though? You brought it to him, didn't you?"

"I did."

"Did you tell him it was a forgery?"

"All I said was, it was identical to the other copies."

"Are you aware of his public statement that the book had been in his family library since he was a kid?"

"If he varnished the truth a little, that's his business."

"After Winthrop learned that Dr. Dunbar and Miss Moore were proofreading the book, did he ever call you and express worry about it?"

"No."

"No?"

"I said no. Ask him about it if you want to."

"We intend to."

"I know what you're after. You don't give a damn who killed who. You're out for the big game. Sling mud. Get Winthrop. Drag him down. Make a name for yourself. Write a book. Make a pile of money."

"I'm not out to get anybody, Mr. Brewner. I'm a cop doing my job."

"All right, you got *me*. Hell, I confess! I'm a criminal! Go ahead, punish me! But you're not going to get at Winthrop through me, so drop it!"

"You're quite loyal to Mr. Winthrop, aren't you?"

"Damn right I am."

"How about your assault on Dr. Dunbar today? What was your motive behind that?"

"If you can't figure that out, you're not much of a detective."

"I can think of reasons, but I'd rather hear it from you."

"Call it revenge on a smart ass. Kerry Arbogast!"

"That's clear enough. Okay, Mr. Brewner, that does it for the time being. I have more questions, but they can wait till we have you booked. Sorry, but I've got to put cuffs on you. Police regulations."

Puterbaugh and Garth led Brewner away.

"Land o' Goshen!" said Goldina. "Talk about drama!"

"You've solved all of it," said Pearl.

"Not me," said Cliff. "Brewner."

"Can you imagine what the newspapers are going to read like next week?" said Akira. "All hell is going to break loose!"

"Know who was the first person to say that?" said Cliff. "John Milton, in *Paradise Lost.*"

"Honey," said Mona, "this is hardly the time to get literary on us."

"Sorry. I'm getting a little woozy. We'd better be off to the hospital."

"I'll drive you," said Mona. "Phil, could you and Akira come along?"

"Of course."

"Hey, Phil," said Cliff, "you did it again! Thanks for pulling me out of that pool!"

"Think nothing of it, Lieutenant. Just bucking for another Silver Star."

"I'll put you in for it, Sergeant."

"But for Pete's sake, Jungle Jim, will you kindly settle down and try to lead a quiet life?"

"I'll see to that," said Mona.

NINETEEN

*T*hey camped in a clearing circled by alders at the water's edge, two or three miles from Whitehorse Rapids on the Deschutes River. The flat-bottomed Deschutes boat, tied to a tree, bobbed in the clear water that lapped against the shore.

Mona's father and Cliff leaned their fly rods against a blackberry bush, sat down on a log, and pulled off their waders. They opened cans of icy beer and lit cigarettes and watched Mona.

Mona had spotted the circles of a feeding ring at one side of a gravel bar in the middle of the stream and waded knee-deep into the water to get away from the trees and gain room for a back cast. She fed out line in two false casts to gain the proper distance and then let the fly line drop onto the water upstream. The tapered monofilament leader fell in the shape of a shepherd's crook, and the Renegade fly, brown and white and iridescent peacock, floated jauntily down the current, turning to left and right, giving the impression of two caddis flies mating. Just as the fly approached the feeding trout, the fly snagged on a floating twig. The trout ignored it.

"Damn!" they heard her exclaim.

On the opposite bank an otter slid into the water. Upstream, an osprey came hurtling down like a dive bomber, hit the surface with its feet, and flew off with an eight-inch trout in its talons. A beam of sunlight came through the trees on the far shore and illuminated Mona's blond curls. Mona executed a snap pickup and cast again.

"Doesn't like to quit, does she, Dave?" said Cliff.

"She loves this river, and she's loved fly fishing ever since she was a kid. I took her on the river as soon as she learned to tie a surgeon's knot and a double turle."

"How old was she then?"

"Seven and a half, and was she a charmer!"

"She still is."

They both looked at her lovingly.

"Something has always puzzled me, Dave. How come women look so trim and fetching in waders and a fly vest, and men look like such scroungy bums?"

"I don't know. It's one of nature's mysteries."

Cliff heaved a sigh and stretched his legs.

"Tired?"

"Yeah. I'm still a little out of shape."

"For a guy who's been shot twice and knifed once, I'd say you're doing all right. . . . Cliff, I ordinarily don't say things like this, but I want to say it once and then we'll forget it: I thank God for you every day."

"Well—thanks."

"Fathers wonder what kind of sons-in-law they'll be stuck with, and Mona's period of adolescent rebellion went into overtime. Did she ever tell you about that musician she took up with?"

"Yes, she did. Seems to have been a sobering experience."

"I couldn't stand the guy. He called me 'man' all the time. He was lazy and infantile and supercilious as hell, but you know what got me most of all? He was a *bad* musician!"

There was a loud splash in the river and Mona called out, "Hurray!" A large, solid rainbow trout shot three feet in the air in a shower of silver drops, angrily shaking its head to get rid of the Renegade in its jaw.

"One of you bring a net, will you?"

Mona fought the trout over to the bank, and Cliff handed her the net. She urged the trout in head first and lifted it out of the water. It was eighteen or nineteen inches long, and deep-bodied—big for the Deschutes.

"Want to keep it for dinner?" her father asked.

"No, it's a spawner. Besides, Cliff and I have agreed to release all of them from here on out." Lowering the fish in the water, she slipped the barbless hook out of its jaw. The trout torpedoed off into the depths.

After dinner, over margaritas around the campfire, Cliff said, "What a magnificent river this is! Mona, if your father and the state of Oregon can stand it, what would you say to our moving up here?"

"I'd love it."

"I'll put in a good word for you with the immigration authorities up in Eugene," said Dave with a grin. "They should be lenient. Neither one of you is a native Californian, after all. You can't help it if the place is overrun with people like Brewner, Collins, Bishop, Flett, Richardson, and Winthrop."

"Let me remind you," said Cliff, "that out of the whole bunch, only Flett and Richardson are natives, and California has put both of them and three of the immigrants in prison. Floretta is with a new bunch of girls in Tehachapi, Collins, Flett, and Richardson are off to Folsom, and Brewner's in Atascadero."

"He's in a what?"

"Atascadero—a prison hospital for the criminally insane."

"How did he work that?"

"Smart lawyer. In a few years he'll suddenly recover his sanity, get out on parole, and flood the state with perfect twenty-dollar bills."

"I still think it stinks, Winthrop rising out of that manure pile with a rose in his teeth."

"That's all he came out with, though. Know what he said when he withdrew from the campaign? 'Although I myself am innocent of any wrongdoing, a leader must take responsibility for the actions of his associates. Otherwise, sheer propinquity could induce the public to misconstrue his motives and question his integrity. I therefore feel that I owe it to the people of California to withdraw my candidacy.'"

"So California won't get its dog races back."

"Nope."

"Shucks. What's Winthrop doing now?"

"He joined a big law firm in Beverly Hills—something like Bigby, Bigby, Higby, Gribble, and Grimes. He'll have the IRS paid off in no time."

" 'Wherefore do the wicked live, and are mighty in power?' "

"And the Mafia rolls on forever."

"Let's go to bed," said Mona. "I'm pooped."

She had zipped their sleeping bags together. They lay close, her head on his shoulder, looking up through the branches of the trees at the stars in the night sky. A cool breeze ruffled her hair. Frogs croaked in the reeds.

"What are you thinking about?" Mona asked.

"Brewner."

"Why him?"

"I feel a kinship with anybody in the world of books and printing. We can't afford to lose people like Brewner. He's such a superb craftsman, and he had everything going for him. I wonder what his tragic flaw was."

"I know what it was."

"What?"

"He was a lousy proofreader."